Prosper Mérimée

Tales Before Supper

Prosper Mérimée

Tales Before Supper

ISBN/EAN: 9783743400634

Manufactured in Europe, USA, Canada, Australia, Japa

Cover: Foto ©Andreas Hilbeck / pixelio.de

Manufactured and distributed by brebook publishing software (www.brebook.com)

Prosper Mérimée

Tales Before Supper

GEMS FROM THE FRENCH

TALES BEFORE SUPPER

FROM

THÉOPHILE GAUTIER

AND

PROSPER MERIMÉE

TOLD IN ENGLISH BY MYNDART VERELST

AND DELAYED WITH A PROEM

BY

EDGAR SALTUS

𝔑𝔢𝔴 𝔜𝔬𝔯𝔨:

BRENTANO'S

PARIS   WASHINGTON   CHICAGO   LONDON

To

E. G. R.

CONTENTS.

INTRODUCTION.

INTRODUCTION.

A SHORT time ago, in the green room of the
Paris Opéra, an old gentleman in an ill-fitting
coat announced to whomsoever would listen
that the most beautiful thing in the world was
a beautiful edition of Gautier. He looked
boldly about as though hoping for a contra-
diction or the chance of an argument, but the
remark passed unchallenged, and nodding sa-
gaciously to himself he went back to the stalls.

The old gentleman perhaps was wrong.
There are, doubtless, many things in the world
more beautiful than that which pleasured his
book-lover fancy, but in literature at least the
number is small. Théophile Gautier is the
Delacroix of prose.

It is related of Anne Boleyn that one of her
eyes was green and the other black. Gautier's
were even more chromatic ; they received and
reflected with the exactitude of a prism every
hue from argent to basaltic. His mental retina
was an oscillating rainbow ; and, were it possible to sum him up in a phrase, it might be said

that of French writers he it was who possessed the clearest perception of color.

Gautier first entered the drawing-room of letters at the age of nineteen. Under his arm he carried a volume of verse. The cover was of pink paper, and its publication had been paid for in advance.

This event occurred in 1830. Romanticism was then at fever heat. Scott had been translated, and, what is more, was being read; Shakespeare had been unearthed; Byron was delighting the world; Goethe glowed in Olympian majesty. It was an era of great deeds, of sonorous adjectives, and exuberant enthusiasm: it was the coming of age of the nineteenth century. It had been found, but a little before, that French literature, if not next door to a pauper, lived practically in the same street. At once the death warrant of classicism was signed. Through the vivifying influence of Chateaubriand, and under the creative hand of Hugo, there leaped into life, as suddenly as the soldiery of Cadmus, a new generation—a race of poets that were virile in their ardor, intoxicated with their own theories, rich in ideas, opulent in fancies, and feverish in the determination to turn the indigence of their country's book shelves into the wealth of a millionnaire. Among them no one was more resolute than Gautier. In aid of the cause he subscribed page after page of luxuriant prose, and line after line of impeccable verse. His ideas were born duchesses. No one could torment a fancy more delicately than he; he had the gift of adjective ; he scented a new one afar like a truffle; and from the Morgue of the dictionary he dragged forgotten beauties. He dowered the language of his day with every tint of dawn and every convulsion of sunset ; he invented metaphors that were worth a king's ransom, and figures of speech that deserve the Prix Montyon. Then, reviewing his work, he formulated an axiom which will go down with a nimbus through time: Whomsoever a thought however complex, a vision however apocalyptic, surprises without words to convey it, is not a writer. The inexpressible does not exist.

When he first set out to charm that gracious lady whose name is Fame, he was as fabulously handsome as a Merovingian prince. He was tall and robust ; his hair was a wayward flood ; his eyes were blue and victorious. He was the image of Young France. His strength was proverbial ; he outdid Danté ; he swam from Marseilles to the Château d'If, and then swam back. Had it been necessary, he would have breasted the Hellespont. But .of that there was no need. There were hearts nearer home that he won without effort ; women fell in love with him at once; the Muse smiled, and

Glory stretched her hand. His conquests were
so numerous that to give an exact account of
them the historian would have to write in
Latin. In comparison Mardoche was a Puri-
tan; and yet, through a charming contradic-
tion, no one has ever been better supplied with
beliefs: he had no less than three hundred and
sixty-five, one for every day in the calendar;
and it was only on leap year that he allowed
himself for twenty-four hours the privilege of
believing in nothing at all.

At a comparatively early age he was sun-
struck by Victor Hugo. To him Hugo was
Phœbus indeed. He has given it to the world
that when he was first brought in the presence, like Esther before Ahasuerus, he almost
swooned. Envy being cheap and the negation
of genius easy, the incident is worth noting;
it helps to an understanding of the man, and of
the poet that was in him. Throughout those
riotous days he was Hugo's henchman. Of the
little army that fought for him, Gautier was the
most demoniac. His contempt of the humdrum, his enthusiasm for the untried, for Liberty in Art, for Hugo, was resplendent in the
fantasy of its ornate charm. To talk poetry
with Hugo, he said, is like talking theology
with God. He did everything for the master.
His pen was a scimitar; his ink, Greek fire;
he defended, lauded, and worshiped. And

when years later, "so many that the head he
bowed had turned to gray," when Hugo came
back from exile, Gautier hastened with a greet-
ing. "Yes," he said on his return, "yes, I
really think he remembered me." Hugo, it
may be noted, rhymes with ego, not richly, perhaps, but well.

Gautier was a satrap of song: as such his
position is not difficult to define. Hugo is the
voice of a century; De Musset the sob; Balzac
the echo; Baudelaire the sneer; and Gautier
the smile,—the smile of youth, health, and good
looks, the smile of one who held aristocracy to
be beauty in woman and intellect in man. He
had little in common with the lyric agony of
De Musset; his hand was not large enough to
wield the thunderbolts which Hugo hurled; he
lacked Baudelaire's appreciation of shades of
leprous brown; and Balzac's stenographic talent was unpossessed by him. But his *facture*
is irreproachable, which De Musset's is not;
his effects are never unintentionally grotesque,
as Hugo's often are; his notes are always natural, where Baudelaire's are sometimes forced;
and, being a poet, it was easier for him to invent than transcribe.

Gautier wrote in verse before he discovered
that it is more difficult to write in prose. Then
abandoning one Muse, he set out to caress the
peplum of another. In this commerce he pro-

duced "Mademoiselle de Maupin," and, later, "Avatar." Concerning "Avatar" little need be said ; the reader is the best of critics. But on the subject of the former work, a momentary digression may perhaps be permitted.

To the average reader "Mademoiselle de Maupin" is a hymn to Love. To the student it is the account of a chase after the Ideal. Through its pages whoso listens hears a strain from Flaubert's immortal duo between Chimera and the Sphinx. That duo in which the crouching beast calls : "Ici, Chimère, arrête-toi," and the Chimera, unstayed in her flight, answers, "Non : jamais."

The Ideal, truly, is intangible, but the fact of its intangibility can hardly be said to make the pursuit other than meritorious. Yet be this as it may, there are many accomplished gentlemen who have thought differently; and in this instance, at least, have called the hunt immoral. The immorality displayed in "Mademoiselle de Maupin" is the tormented grace of adolescence, the emotion which stirs the pulse of every youth however refined, and every maiden however pure. It represents the turbulence of health, the love of beauty, and the unaffected expression of a sentiment which while perfectly natural has the misfortune to shock those who lack the ability to inspire it in another. It is a tableau of the candors and generous dreams that reside in every one who prefers the beautiful to its opposite. As such, perhaps, it is immoral, though one may wonder in what the criterion consists; and it may not be indecorous to note that they who declaim on the subject are sometimes at a loss for a standard or an instance of morality in nature. Besides, Gautier did not write for accomplished gentlemen, nor yet for little girls in short frocks. He wrote for poets and for men. And where is the poet who would not envy d'Albert, and where is the man who would not have kissed the fair Madeleine? For my part, were the permission accorded me, I know of nothing that could give me greater pleasure. No, not even a conversation with Schopenhauer.

But to preach liberality to the illiberal is, as we all know, as profitable as asking alms of statues. Then, too, who shall question taste? The perfume which is distressing to one is alluring to another. The concert which delights the idler is painful to the amateur. The secret of never displeasing is the art of mediocrity. And Gautier alternately charms and rebuffs. His Muse has a thousand toilettes ; she lives in a succession of masquerades. At times she moves in a minuet. Again she comes with the breath of brooks and sorceries of spring; now she is enveloped in the incense and hallelujahs of a cathedral, now in the fireworks and frenzy of a debauch; to-day a princess, yesterday a vagrant, to-morrow a wanton, last week a saint —but always the Muse.

If her attitude in "Mademoiselle de Maupin" may be considered venturesome, no such reproach has been laid at the door of "Avatar." There the heroine is endowed with a purity so tremulous in its clairvoyance that the Blessed Damozel herself might have envied it, and not she alone, but the

> . . . five handmaidens whose names
> Are five sweet symphonies :
> Cecily, Gertrude, Magdalen,
> Margaret and Rosalys.

Prascovie Labinska is meet to be reckoned with such as they, and the portrait which Gautier drew of her could have been signed by no one else save perhaps Guido or Carlo Dolci. In this story he succeeded in what few have accomplished before,—he displayed the impalpable on paper, a dream in black and white. The reader assists at a metamorphosis more marvelous than any Paracelsus ever devised. A forenoon of Veronese fades as in a magic lantern; in its place comes a tableau after Goya, a nightmare of the Orient in modern guise, a picture of the human soul fluttering as might a bird over the horrors of an abyss. And then, at once, the dawn.

Gautier had a taste for the exotic, and he

toyed with it as with a jewel. His knowledge was something wider than encyclopædic; he was familiar with the odds and ends of learning, the remnants and misfits of erudition; he knew the reason of things, and confused many whose business in life was to seem wise without being so. In latter years no one knew when he slept. His lamp was always burning. When he rested it was with a book. One day, so runs the legend,[1] he happened to be visiting at a country house. His fellow-guests were artists and savants. Near the house was a pond stocked with immemorial carp. Somebody suggested that one of these fish might be appetizing for breakfast. Accordingly a carp was caught and carried to the kitchen. Suddenly the head cook, his face whiter than his cap, and followed by trembling scullions, appeared among the assembled guests. In a voice broken by emotion he announced that the carp had no sooner been placed in the pot than the · most heart-rending cries had come from it. The scullions bore witness to the truth of this statement, and declared that they would rather resign their aprons than be obliged to assist at the cooking of such an extraordinary fish.

"Extraordinary!" said Gautier," not at all. All fish object to being boiled alive. The carp merely happened to have a stronger voice than the others."

[1] *Théophile Gautier.* Emile Bergerat. · Paris.

At this remark of the poet's, the savants were vastly amused. Nothing, they said, was better established than that fish were dumb. The cook evidently had been mystified or deceived by some illusion of the acoustics. Besides, they insisted, how can fish cry out,— they have no vocal organs?

"Forgive me," said Gautier, "they have." And thereupon he gave the assembly such a lesson in ichthyology that it seemed as though all the fish of the rivers and the oceans protested with him against the ignorance of man. He dissected and anatomized the finest fibres of their vocal organs. He made them vibrate, sing, cry, and murmur according to their joy or pain. He unveiled their mysterious lives, their loves, their wars, and touching at last on the abominable torture which is inflicted on them when they are cooked alive, he pictured it in such terms that Bergerat says even the scullions wept, and of the guests not one could be induced to touch fish for over a week.

The next day one of the erudites who had returned to Paris wrote to Gautier: "I have passed the night in verifying your assertions; every one of them is exact. It is you who are the savant and we who are poets."

It was this readiness that he brought to his work. Wit and wisdom ran off the end of his pen, and in the running assumed such per-

fect attitudes that Balzac, whose own phrases
were laborious as childbirth, called him a magician, which he undoubtedly was. The quality of his style has been rarely questioned.
Zola, it is true, has characterized it as tortured,
and were it not malicious to wish that the style
of that Jupiter Feuilletonant could be put on
the same rack, the wish most assuredly would
be expressed. But Zola to the contrary, Gautier so far from tormenting his style, did not
even polish it. The secret of his grace and
fluency lay, perhaps, in this. His mind was a
kaleidoscope of fancies; he had but to shake
it and an alluring combination was the result.
Moreover, his memory was like a vise. It was
never necessary for him to look up a refer-
ence; the dictionary was a relaxation to him;
and when he wrote, — and he wrote everything, from an epigram to a ballet, enough, in
fact, to fill a library, — the operation was absolutely painless. None of his manuscripts bear
the slightest trace of revision, of erasure, or,
for that matter, of punctuation. Bergerat says
that after an interruption, such as a visit for
instance, he would take up his work at the
place he left off, often in the middle of a word,
without so much as refreshing his memory by
a reading of the sentence that preceded it.
He wrote a sonnet as readily as an acceptance
to a dinner, a story as easily as were he copy-

ing it. He wrote an acrostic sonnet, *bout-rimé* at that — one of the most difficult things in verse — as an improvisation. He went to Russia, and four years later, without a note-book to help him, wrote a description of what he had seen. The "Capitaine Fracasse," one of his chief works, a story of sixteenth century France, in which there is not an anachronism of language or of detail, was written at the end of a counter in a publisher's office, without even a lexicon at hand, amid the confusion of a large establishment, and as the manuscript fell from him it was carried to the printer. When the printer had enough for the day, Gautier took a stroll in the boulevard. Certainly he was a magician.

Beside the book of Russian travels, Gautier wrote another on Spain. It was alleged that he grazed the surface of things, and left the backgrounds unpenetrated. "Théo," said that delightful Mme. de Girardin one evening, "are there no Russians in Russia, no Spaniards in Spain ?"

At this Gautier pretended to be very angry. "Fiddlesticks !" he exclaimed, or rather the Gallic equivalent. "Do you suppose I saw them ? In St. Petersburg I was a Russian my-self, in Madrid I was as thorough a Spaniard as the Cid or Don Ruy Gomez de Silva. I no sooner put my foot in a country than I

become a native, I think, act, and see precisely
like any other inhabitant. In Spain I would
have had myself run through and through in
defense of any one of a dozen different local
opinions, no matter which, provided my sword
had been tempered at Toledo, and the challenge was addressed to Don Theophilo. As
to Russian customs, I adopted them at once.
I adopted them as a matter of course; I forgot all others that differed. To me they seemed
perfectly natural. Would you think of describing the form of a cravat in a land where every
cravat is of the same form? No. Well, then,
no more would I. Beside, man is everywhere
the same. In every latitude he eats with his
mouth and grasps with his fingers. No matter
where you go you will find that the strong overcome the weak. From one pole to the other
the art of love does not vary. To my thinking,
descriptions of habits and customs are not worth
the stroke of a pen; personally, I care as much
for them as I do for the snows of yester-year.
I have passed my life in a pursuit of the Beautiful, and I found it only in Nature and in Art.
Everywhere and always man is ugly. He
spoils creation. His sole value is in his intelligence. And as his intelligence is manifest
only in his productions, I hold but to them;
the secret of his destinies does not interest me
in the least. The one thing that I care about

in a foreign city is, therefore, the monuments, and I care for them simply because they convey the collective result of the genius of the population. If the population be brutal and the city a haunt of crime, what does it matter to me? All I ask is the permission to admire the edifices without being assassinated. As for humanity as it is improperly called, there is the 'Gazette des Tribunaux,' the 'Newgate Calendar;' all Balzac is in it, and over and above Balzac the universal history of that mischievous ape that I have met in all my travels, and who peoples the world. That is the way it is, and that is the way it always will be. It is only climates that differ, climates, thieves-slang, and the uniform of the police."

After this tirade it is probable that he shrugged his shoulders and repeated the favorite axiom of his declining years, " There is no use in anything ; and, moreover, there is nothing ; yet everything happens, but to me it is all the same." An axiom which, heard in conjunction with the foregoing tirade, might be mistaken for the purest Leopardi. But Gautier was anything but a miserabilist. Indifference makes one good-natured. In his youth he was too magnificent to be other than happy, and in his old age too sweet-tempered to believe in discontent.

Such change as there was in his disposition

was that which is the outcome of Time. As a young man he promenaded the boulevards in wonderful trousers, transcendent waistcoats, neckclothed like Brummel, gazing about with conquering eyes. In the majestic indolence of later years he looked much as might an Asiatic potentate grown gray and grave. Victory had deserted his eyes, and in them had come a shadowy nostalgia, the regret of unsailed seas and unexperienced pleasures, and therewith a reverie so feline in its abstraction that one might have thought him constantly following the changes of some unending dream.

And that dream was, of course, the Beautiful. In the first intoxication of romanticism he caught the Muse by the hair, and threw her down like a young ruffian felling his mistress; he was vigorous in his beliefs, but as illusions left him, as illusions do, he intercepted some knowledge of the intangibility of the Ideal, and it was then that he shrugged his shoulders. Enthusiasm for a chimera is indeed difficult to prolong.

The story of the "Venus of Ille" is by an author of a different school. Prosper Mérimée was in a certain sense even more erudite than Gautier. He was a professional archæologist, an historian salaried by the state, a *fumiste* of literature, one of the mandarins of the Occident — that is to say, a member of the French

Academy, — a senator to boot, and at Saint Cloud and the Tuileries the modern representative of the jester of the past. Though he wore no bells, his business was none the less to amuse the court. He wrote witty little comedies, which were performed by titled amateurs, and to the empress he whispered anecdotes behind the fan.

His lines were cast in pleasant places. In after-life Gautier had to trudge through journalism, a martyr to the exigencies of the daily press, but Mérimée wore a braided coat, and drew an income from the coffers of the crown. He was rarely gifted, a man of sound learning, a philologist to the ends of his gloves, a student in the true acceptation of the word, and yet one who not from modesty but diplomacy preferred to be thought a dilettante. He did not wish to seem wiser than dukes and duchesses. Throughout his literary career he acted like that Englishman who refused to speak French correctly that he might not be taken for a professor of languages. He wrote a bundle of excellent verse, " La Guzla," which he published as translations from the Illyrian, and which were gravely commented upon by spectacled Germans. He produced a volume of plays, which he gave out as translations from an imaginary Spanish actress, Clara Gazul, whose manuscripts he pretended to have found when rummaging in the Escurial. The plays were strikingly original, nervous in movement, colorless in adjective, unburdened by an unnecessary word, and in peculiar contrast to the exuberance and fervor of the day. They too were gravely commented upon, and long articles were written about Clara Gazul and the art which that lady displayed.

Mérimée meanwhile laughed in his sleeve. Somebody, Taine perhaps, has said that his existence was dual. When the Mérimée whom the world knew showed himself in public, the real Mérimée stood at his side, and with an air of mockery resignedly watched him perform.

The Mérimée that the world knew was a pale impassible man, who never raised his voice, who said clever things, and told horrible stories with the impersonal unconcern of one describing the fair weather of an earlier June. It was said that he was an atheist, or, what is worse, a materialist, that he was without sentiment, without affection, without a heart. But after the posthumous publication of his " Lettres à une Inconnue," it was discovered that he had worn a mask, it was found that he had beliefs, nay, superstitions even, and that his heart could bleed as well as another. The pale impassible erudite disappeared, and in his place came an unknown Mérimée, a lover, tender, delicate, and always refined, who wrote to the Inconnue lines like these : —

"It is so long since I heard from you that I had begun to be anxious. Besides, I was tormented with a presentiment that I have not dared to relate. A few days ago I went with an architect to the Arenas of Nîmes, and there, ten paces from me, I noticed a charming bird. It was a trifle larger than a lark, its body was the color of flax, and its wings were striated black, white, and crimson. It was perched on a cornice, and gazed fixedly at me. I interrupted the architect to ask what kind of bird it was: although a great sportsman, he said that never before had he seen one like it. I went up to it, but it did not attempt to fly until I was near enough to touch it with my hand. Then, with its eyes still fixed on me, it fluttered a little distance away. Wherever I went, it followed me. The next day I returned to the Arenas, and found the bird still there. I had brought some bread with me, but it would not touch it. Thinking from the form of its beak that it might prefer insects, I threw it a grasshopper, but it paid no attention to it. The foremost ornithologist of the town told me that no such bird as I described had ever been seen in the neighborhood. Finally, at my last visit to the Arenas, the bird followed me so persistently that it even came after me into a dark passage which only a bat would have entered. I remembered then that the Duchess of Buckingham saw her husband in the form of a bird on the day that he was assassinated, and at once I feared that you had died, and had taken that way of seeing me. In spite of myself, the idea was torment, and I assure you I was delighted to see that your letter bore the date of the day on which I first saw my marvelous bird."

So much for the poet that the world did not know.

As a rule, when the real Mérimée showed himself it was in spheres unfrequented by fashion, over the gourd of a galley-slave for instance, in a nest of gitanas, or in some smuggler's haunt. Gautier, it may be remembered, discovered Andalusia, and every one since has wished to follow in his footsteps. The journey can be made in different ways. The pleasantest, perhaps, is by means of that enchanted rug, the imagination. A history aiding, one or two books of travel, and it is the easiest thing in the world to explore the entire land without so much as leaving one's arm-chair. The traveler closes his eyes, and presto! the Alhambra, the Lion Court, the Alcazar, Cordova, the ship of stone which is called Cadiz, surge in melting beauty before him. On the wings of his vagabond fancy he can float from Carthagena to Tyre ; he can see the Phœnicians sailing in their purple galleys ; he can hear the tramp of Roman soldiery ; he can scan the face

of Cæsar, vicious and blanched by incessant
debauches; he can watch the inundation of the
Vandals, the conquest of the Goths, the glitter
of the Mussulman scimiter, and if his ear be
properly attuned, he can catch the tinkle of the
Moorish guitar. The ages will unveil their secrets, the cities their gore and their charm,
and all this without being forced to ask a deaf
man suffering from a cold at what time the
train starts. This is, perhaps, the usual plan,
though another and equally patriotic fashion is
to go there ignorant of Spanish, ignorant of
history, and after cursing the country long to
be at home.

Prosper Mérimée chose none of these ways.
The obscurest corner of history was his by
right of conquest. He not only spoke Spanish,
he spoke the *calo* of the gypsies and the jargon
of the Catalans. When, therefore, the fancy
took him to visit Andalusia, he went there in
the directest manner. Few were the doors
closed to him. He ate and drank with the
best, with the Duke of Ossuna, whose ancestor
Geryon tended the flocks of the Sun; with
Mme. de Montijo, mother of the empress that
was to be; and when his evening dress was put
aside, and the Mérimée that the world knew was
supposed to be asleep, he was supping in some
fonda that reeked with garlic, chatting with
muleteers and chulos, telling stories to the

peasants of Ronda, lounging under the stars with smugglers and highwaymen, or watching some drama of jealousy, that jealousy that spends itself not in a scene, but in a murder. From these and similar excursions he brought back the portraits that fill his gallery. Carmen, for instance, Columba, and Cleménce. They are all living, not one of them has stepped into a book before, and yet with five or six strokes of the pen he makes the reader as familiar with them as were they stock characters of fiction. It was this method that he observed wheresoever he went, and as he was a great traveler the variety of his types is noticeable.

These portraits are hung in the plainest frames. After Gautier, the sobriety of his style is ascetic. To turn from " Avatar " to the "Venus of Ille " is like passing from high noon to twilight. The action in both is as sinewy as it is dramatic ; so far as the mere management is concerned one is at a loss to decide which is the more nervous ; but while through " Avatar " one can hear Gautier's voice, see his ample gestures, mark the forgetfulness of his volubilities, and feel as did one sit with him hand in hand that the tale is told with really personal sympathy, one looks in vain through the " Venus of Ille " for the faintest trace of emotion.

Mérimée has a story to tell, and he tells it as though he were giving evidence before a

grand jury.   He presents facts, not hearsay;
each word of his testimony is relevant; he is
not to be led into confusion or entangled in
contradictions.   He is logical, precise, plain-
spoken, and undeclamatory.   A perfect witness
indeed.   No one in all probability will ever be
able to write as richly as Gautier, but in Mérimée's stories may be discerned the model of
the modern novel — the art of displaying the
documents in a given case uninterruptedly, one
after the other like so many premises with a
conclusion for climax.   Gautier was the torch
of an epoch, Mérimée the rapier.

                                        EDGAR SALTUS.
NEW YORK, *May* 1, 1887.

AVATAR.

AVATAR.

BY THÉOPHILE GAUTIER.

I.

No one could understand the malady which
was slowly undermining Octave de Saville.
He was not confined to his bed; his ordinary
existence was unchanged; no complaint fell
from his lips; and yet it was none the less evident that he was fading away. Questioned
by the physicians whom the solicitations of his
friends and relations forced him to consult, he
could mention no definite suffering, nor could
science discover an alarming symptom: the
auscultation of the chest gave out a favorable
sound, and the ear applied to the heart de-
tected scarcely an irregular pulsation; he had
neither cough nor fever, but life ebbed from
him through one of those invisible rents of
which, Terence says, man is full.

Sometimes a strange faintness made him
white as marble, for a few moments he appeared lifeless, then the pendulum, no longer

stopped by the mysterious finger which had held it, resumed its sway, and Octave awakened as from a dream.

He had been sent to a water-cure, but the thermal nymphs proved powerless to help him, and a journey to Naples produced no better re-sult. The radiant sun, of which he had heard so much, was to him as black as Albert Dürer has engraved it; the bat with Melancholia writ-ten on its wing beat the dazzling sky with its dusky web, and flew between him and the light; on the quay of Mergellina, where the half-clad lazzaroni sun themselves till their skins take on the hue of bronze, he had felt chilled to the heart. So returning to his small apartment in the Rue Saint - Lazare, he had apparently resumed his former habits.

This apartment was for a bachelor most comfortably furnished. But as in time an in-terior becomes impressed with the look and even the very thought of its inhabitant, Oc-tave's home had little by little grown dull and mournful; the damask curtains had faded and admitted but a gray light; the large bunches of flowers were withering on the dingy white of the carpet; the gilt frames of a few choice water-colors and sketches had slowly reddened under a relentless dust; a discouraged fire smoked and died out under its own ashes; the antique buhl clock, inlaid with brass and tortoise shell, withheld the noise of its tick-tack, and the voice of the dreary hours spoke low as one does in a sick-room; the doors closed silently, and the footfalls of rare visitors died away on the thick carpet; laughter ceased on penetrating these cold, sombre rooms, wherein modern luxury was omnipresent. Octave's servant, Jean, a duster under his arm, a tray in his hand, glided about like a shadow, for, unconsciously, affected by the surrounding gloom, he had ended by losing his natural loquacity. Trophies, such as boxing gloves, masks, and foils, hung on the walls, but it was easy to see that they had long been untouched; books were tossed carelessly about, as if Octave had tried to lull some fixed idea by mechanical reading. An unfinished letter, yellowed with age, seemed to have been waiting its conclusion for months, and spread itself out on the table in silent reproach. Though inhabited, the apartment appeared deserted. Life was absent, and on entering one encountered the chill which issues from a tomb. In this lugubrious dwelling, where no woman ever set her foot, Octave was more at his ease than elsewhere; the silence, the sadness, and the neglect suited him; the joyous tumult of life disgusted him, though he made frequent efforts to join in it; but as he returned from the masquerades, the balls, or the suppers to which his friends dragged him, gloomier than before, he struggled no longer against his mysterious pain, and let the days slip by with the indifference of a man who expects nothing from the morrow.   As he had lost faith in the future he made no plans, and having tacitly sent in his resignation to life, he was awaiting its acceptance.   Nevertheless, if you imagined him thin of face, with an earthy complexion, attenuated limbs, and a wasted appearance, you would be much mistaken ; a dark bruise under the eyelids, an orange shade around the orbits, a hollowing of the temples veined with blue, were alone observable.   Yet his eyes were soulless, without trace of will, hope, or desire.   This lifeless gaze in such a young face formed a strange contrast, and produced a more painful effect than the emaciated features and fevered expression of the ordinary invalid.   Before his health was affected in this way Octave had been called a good-looking fellow, and he was so still ; thick, wavy black hair clustered in silky, lustrous masses at his temples ; his eyes were large, velvety, and deeply blue, fringed with curved lashes, and at times luminous with a liquid fire ; in repose, and when unanimated by passion, they had the serene look which the eyes of Orientals wear when, after smoking their nargileh, they take their *kief* at the café doors of Smyrna or Constantinople.   His skin, always pale, had that southern tint of olive white which is most effective by gaslight; his hand was slender and delicate ; his foot narrow and arched. He dressed well, without being in advance of the fashion or behind it, and knew perfectly how to set off his natural attractions to their best advantage. Though without the pretensions of an exquisite or a sportsman, had he been put up at the Jockey Club he would not have been blackballed.

How was it, then, that a man, young, handsome, rich, with every incentive to happiness, should be thus miserably consuming himself ? The reader will imagine that Octave was blasé, that the novels of the day had filled his brain with morbid ideas, that he had no beliefs, that of his youth and fortune squandered in dissipation nothing remained to him but debts. All these suppositions would be erroneous. Octave had seen too little of dissipation to be tired of it : neither splenetic, romantic, atheistic, nor libertine, his life had been that of the average young man, a commingling of study and relaxation. In the morning, lectures at the Sorbonne claimed his attention, and in the evening, he might be seen stationed on the staircase of the Opéra watching the tide of beauty disperse. He was not known to take interest in either actress or duchess, and he spent his income without encroaching on the principal, — his

lawyer respected him! In brief, he was of
an equable temperament, incapable of jumping off a precipice, or setting a river on fire.
The cause of his condition, which baffled the
skill of the entire faculty, was so incredible in
nineteenth century Paris that we must leave its
narration to our hero.

As the ordinary scientists could make nothing of this strange illness (at the amphitheatres of anatomy a soul has yet to be dissected),
an eccentric physician recently returned from
India, and reputed to effect marvelous cures,
was consulted as a last resource.

Octave, foreseeing a superior discernment
capable of penetrating his secret, seemed to
dread the doctor's visit, and it was only after
repeated entreaties from his mother that he
consented to receive M. Balthazar Cherbonneau. When the physician entered, Octave was
stretched on a sofa; his head was propped up
by a cushion, another supported his elbow, and
a third covered his feet: wrapped in the soft
and supple folds of a Turkish gown, he was
reading, or rather holding, a book, for his eyes,
though fixed on a page, saw nothing. His face
was colorless, but, as has been hinted, showed
no marked alteration. A superficial examination would not have disclosed dangerous symptoms in this young invalid, on whose table,
instead of the pills, vials, potions, and other

drugs usual in such cases, stood a box of
cigars. Though slightly drawn, his clear-cut
features had lost little of their natural charm,
and but for his extreme debility and the irre-
mediable despondency of his eye Octave would
have appeared in a normal state of health.

In spite of his apathy Octave was struck
by the physician's fantastic appearance. M.
Balthazar Cherbonneau seemed as though he
had escaped from one of Hoffmann's Tales,
and was wandering about astounded at the
reality of his own grotesqueness. His sunburnt face was overhung by an enormous skull,
which loss of hair made appear even larger
than it really was. The bald cranium, polished
as ivory, had remained white, while the face,
exposed to the rays of the sun, had taken on
the color of old oak or a smoky portrait. Its
cavities and projecting bones were thrown in
such bold relief that their slight covering of
wrinkled flesh resembled damp parchment
stretched on a death's-head. The infrequent
gray hairs which still lingered on the back of
the head were gathered in three thin locks,
— two drawn up over the ears, and the third,
starting from the nape of the neck and ending abruptly at the beginning of the forehead,
crowned this nut-cracker countenance, and
evoked unconscious regrets for the ancient
peruque or the modern wig. But the most

extraordinary thing about him was his eyes.
His face, wrinkled with age, calcinated by incandescent skies, worn with vigils, marked in
lines more closely pressed than the pages of a
book, with the wearisome fatigues of life and
of study, was illuminated by two orbs of turquoise blue, inconceivably limpid, fresh, and
youthful. Sunken in sombre sockets, whose
concentric membranes and pink edges vaguely
recalled the dilating and contracting pupils
of an owl, they gleamed like two blue stars,
and made one suspect that, aided by some
witchery of the Brahmans, the physician had
stolen the eyes of a child, and transplanted
them to his own cadaverous visage. Octave's
eyes were those of an octogenarian, but Cherbonneau's blazed with the fire of youth. He
was dressed in the physician's ordinary garb,
a suit of black with silk waistcoat of the same
color, while his shirt-front was ornamented with
a large diamond, the present of some rajah or
nabob. But, as if suspended from a peg, his
clothes hung on him in perpendicular folds,
broken, when he was seated, into sharp angles
by his limbs. India's devouring sun could
hardly have been the only cause of the phe-
nomenal emaciation which he exhibited. It
may be that in view of some initiation he had
undergone the prolonged fasts of the fakirs,
and had been extended by the yogis between

four glowing braziers on the skin of a gazelle. His attenuation, however, was not the outcome of debility. His fleshless knuckles moved noiselessly, as were they held together by strong ligaments stretched on the hands like the strings of a violin.

With a stiff movement of the elbows which resembled the folding of a yard-measure, the physician seated himself in the chair by the sofa to which Octave motioned him, betraying, as he did so, an inveterate habit of squatting on a mat. So placed, M. Cherbonneau's back was turned to the light which fell directly on the face of his patient, a situation most favorable to examination, and one usually chosen by observers more desirous of seeing than of being seen. Though the physician's face was hidden in shadow, and the top of his cranium, round and polished as a gigantic ostrich-egg, alone caught a ray of light, Octave discerned the scintillation of his singular blue pupils, which appeared endowed with the glimmer peculiar to phosphorescent bodies, and emitted a clear, sharp beam which penetrated the invalid's chest with the hot, pricking sensation which an emetic causes.

"Well, sir," said the physician after a moment's silence, during which he seemed to sum up the symptoms noted in his rapid inspection, "I see already that yours is not a case of every-day pathology. You have none of the well-known signs of catalogued maladies which the physician cures or aggravates ; and I shall not ask you for paper, or write from the codex a soothing prescription with a hieroglyphical signature for tail-piece, or trouble your servant to go to the corner drug-shop." Octave smiled faintly as if to thank M. Cherbonneau for sparing him useless and disagreeable remedies.

" But," resumed the physician, "do not rejoice too quickly ; because you have neither heart-disease, consumption, spinal complaint, softening of the brain, typhoid or nervous fever, it does not follow that you are in good health. Give me your hand."

Thinking M. Cherbonneau wished to count his pulse, and expecting to see him take out his watch for that purpose, Octave drew back the sleeve of his dressing-gown, and baring his wrist extended it mechanically. Into his yellow paw, of which the bony fingers resembled the claws of a crab, M. Cherbonneau took the young man's moist, veined hand, but instead of feeling with his thumb for that uneven pulsation which indicates that the machinery of man is out of order, he pressed and kneaded it as if to put himself in magnetic communication with his subject.

Though a skeptic in medicine, Octave could not restrain a sort of anxious emotion. The blood receded from his temples, and it seemed to him as if the physician's pressure was subtracting his very soul.

"My dear sir," M. Cherbonneau said, as he dropped Octave's hand, "your condition is far graver than you think ; the old-fashioned treatments that are in vogue in Europe cannot aid you in the least. You have lost the will to live ; insensibly, your soul is slipping from your body; yet there is no trace of hypochondria, lymphomania, nor yet of melancholy and suicidal preoccupation. No ! There is nothing of that. Strange as it may appear, you might, did I not prevent you, succumb suddenly, without a single noticeable rupture internal or external. It is high time that I was summoned, for your spirit holds to your body merely by a thread ; we will make a good strong knot of it, however." And therewith the doctor rubbed his hands blithesomely together, and smiled in a manner that sent the wrinkles eddying through the thousand lines of his weather-worn face.

"Monsieur Cherbonneau," Octave answered, "I do not know whether you will succeed, and as to that I care very little ; but I must admit that you have gauged the cause of my mysterious affliction in the exactest and most penetrating manner. I feel as though I had become permeable, as though I were losing my ego as water runs through a sieve. I am

melting away into the universal essence, and
it is with difficulty that I distinguish my own
identity from the surroundings into which it is
being fused. Life, of which, as well as may
be, I perform the daily pantomime to avoid
grieving my relatives and friends, seems so far
from me that there are moments when I feel
as if I had already left this mortal sphere.
Actuated by habitual motives whose mechanical impulse still lingers, I come and go, but
without participating in my own actions. At
the usual hours I seat myself at table, and appear to eat and drink; but the most highly sea-
soned dishes and the strongest wines have no
flavor to me. The sunshine is pale as moonlight, and candle-flames are dark. I shiver in
midsummer. Often an intense silence op-
presses me, much as though my heart had
ceased beating, and the wheelwork was clogged
by some unknown cause. If the dead are sen-
tient, my condition must resemble theirs."

"You have," replied the physician, "a
chronic inability to live, an entirely moral
disease, and one more frequent than is supposed. Thought is a force which can kill as
surely as electricity or prussic acid, though the
signs of its ravages cannot be grasped by the
means of such analysis as is at the disposal of
vulgar science. What sorrow has set its fangs
in your heart? From what secretly ambitious

height have you fallen crushed and broken?
On what despair do you muse in your immobility? Is it the thirst for power which tor-
ments you? Have you voluntarily renounced
an aim placed too high for human attainment?
You are very young for that. May it be that
a woman has betrayed you?"

"No, doctor," continued Octave; "I have
not even enjoyed that happiness."

"And yet," continued M. Balthazar Cherbonneau, "in your dull eyes, in the listless attitude
of your body, in the lifeless tones of your voice,
I read, as plainly as if it were stamped in gold
letters on a morocco binding, the title of one
of Shakespeare's plays."

"And what is this play which I unconsciously
translate?" asked Octave, whose curiosity was
aroused in spite of himself.

"Love's Labor's Lost," continued the doctor,
with a purity of accent which betrayed a long
residence in the English colonies of India.

Octave did not answer; a slight blush reddened his cheeks, and to cover his embarrassment he toyed with the tassel of his girdle.
The physician crossed one leg over the other,
producing the effect of the crossbones carved
on tombs, and clasped his foot in his hand in
Oriental fashion. His blue eyes gazed into
Octave's with a look at once soft and imperious.

"Come, come," said M. Balthazar Cherbonneau, "confide in me; souls are my specialty; you are my patient; and, like the Catholic priest to the penitent, I ask for a complete confession, and you can make it without kneeling."

"What good would it do? Supposing that you have divined correctly, the telling of my affliction would not relieve it. My sorrow is dumb. No earthly power, not even yours, can cure me."

"Perhaps," said the physician, settling himself more comfortably in his arm-chair, as if preparing to listen to a long confidence.

"I do not wish you," continued Octave, "to accuse me of a puerile obstinacy, nor to give you by my silence a pretext for washing your hands of my death; so, since you ask it, I will tell you my history: you have guessed the main point, I need not spare the details. Do not expect anything singular or romantic. It is a very simple adventure, very commonplace, very threadbare; but, as sings Henri Heine, whoso meets it finds it ever new, though the heart be broken every time. Really, I am ashamed to relate such an ordinary tale to a man who has lived in the most fabulous and chimerical countries."

"Do not fear," said the physician, smiling, "it is only the commonplace which can be extraordinary to me."

"Well, doctor, love is killing me."

II.

"TOWARDS the end of the summer of 184–,
I found myself in Florence, at the best season for seeing that city. I had time, money,
excellent letters of introduction, and I was a
good-humored youth, only too ready to be
amused. I installed myself on the Lung'-
Arno, hired a trap, and drifted into that easy
Florentine life which is so full of charm to the
stranger. In the morning I visited some
church, palace, or gallery, quite leisurely, without hurry, as I did not wish to give myself
that indigestion of master - pieces which dis-
gusts the too hasty tourist with art. One
morning I examined the bronze doors of the
Baptistery; another, the Perseus of Benvenuto
under the Loggia dei Lanzi, the portrait of
Fornarina, or Canova's Venus in the Pitti Palace, but never more than one object at a
time. Then I breakfasted off a cup of iced
coffee at the Café Doney, smoked a cigar or
two, glanced at the papers, and, my bottonhole
decorated, willingly or not, by one of the pretty
flower-girls who in their huge straw hats stand
before the café, I returned home for a siesta.
At three o'clock the carriage came to take me
to the Cascine. The Cascine is to Florence
what the Bois de Boulogne is to Paris, with

this difference, that every one is acquainted,
and the square is an open-air drawing-room,
where chairs are replaced by the half circle of
carriages. The women, in full dress, recline on
the cushions, and receive the visits of lovers,
friends, exquisites, and attachés, who pose, hat
in hand, at the carriage-steps. But you know
all this as well as I. There plans for the
evening are made, meetings are arranged,
answers are given, invitations accepted; it is
like a Pleasure Exchange open from three to
five in the shade of beautiful trees, under the
world's fairest sky. It is incumbent on every
one of the least consequence to be seen there
daily, and I was careful not to miss it. In the
evening I made a visit or two, or if the prima
donna was an attraction I went to the Pergola.

"In this way I spent one of the happiest
months of my life; but my good fortune was
not destined to last. One day a magnificent
open carriage made its first appearance at
the Cascine. It was one of Laurenzi's *chef-
d'œuvres*, and a superb example of Viennese
manufacture; glittering with varnish, and blazoned with an almost royal coat of arms, there
was harnessed to it as handsome a pair of
horses as ever paraded in Hyde Park, or drew
up before Saint James' Palace during a drawing-room; added to this, it was driven à la Dau-
mont in the correctest style by a youthful pos-

tilion in green livery and white knee-breeches. The brass on the harness, the boxes of the wheels, the door-handles, all shone like gold and sparkled in the sun; every eye followed this splendid equipage, which, after making a curve as regular as if traced by a compass, drew up near the other vehicles. The carriage, you may be sure, was not empty; but in the speed with which it passed nothing had been distinguished but the tip of a slipper extended on a cushion, a large fold of shawl, and the disk of a parasol fringed with white silk. The parasol was now closed, and a woman of incomparable beauty was revealed. Being on horseback, I was able to approach near enough to lose no detail of this poem in flesh. The fair stranger, with the assurance of a perfect blonde, wore a gown of that silvery Nile green which makes any woman whose skin is not irreproachable look as dark as that of a mole. A beautiful shawl of white crêpe de Chine, thick with embroidery of the same color, enveloped her like a Phidian statue in its clinging, rumpled drapery, while a bonnet of fine Florentine straw, covered with forget-me-nots and delicate aquatic plants of slender glaucous leaves, formed an aureole about her face. Her only ornament was a gold lizard studded with turquoises, which encircled the arm that held the parasol.

"Forgive me, doctor, this fashion-plate description. To a lover these trivialities are of enormous importance. Thick, rippling golden hair lay like undulations of light in luxuriant waves upon her brow, which itself was smooth and white as the new-fallen snow on the highest Alpine peak; long lashes, fine as the threads of gold radiating from the angel heads in the miniatures of the Middle Ages, veiled her eyes, whose pupils had the bluish-green light of a sun-pierced glacier. Her divinely modeled mouth glowed with the carmine of a sea-shell, and her cheeks resembled white roses flushed by the wooing of the nightingale or the kiss of the butterfly; no mortal brush could copy the suavity, the fairness, and the immaterial transparency of this complexion, of which the tints seemed hardly due to the blood which colors our coarser skins; the first blush of morn on the ridge of the Sierra Nevada, the rose-tipped petals of a camellia, Parian marble seen through a pink gauze veil, can alone give of it a vague idea. The creamy iridescence of the neck, visible between the shawl and the bonnet strings, gleamed with opalescent reflections. It was the Venetian coloring, and not the features, that arrested attention, though the latter were as clear cut and exquisite as the profile of an antique cameo. When I saw her, I forgot my past loves, as Romeo at sight of

Juliet forgot Rosalind. The pages of my heart
became blank : every name, every memory, was
obliterated. I wondered how the commonplace love affairs which few young men escape
had ever had any attraction for me, and I re-
proached myself for them as if they had been
culpable infidelities. A new life dated for me
from this fatal encounter.

" Presently the carriage left the Cascine and
took the road back to town. When the dazzling vision had vanished I brought my horse
alongside that of an amiable young Russian, a
great lover of watering places, a man who had
frequented all the cosmopolitan drawing-rooms
of Europe, and who was thoroughly conversant
with the traveling contingent of high life ; I
turned the conversation on the fair stranger,
and learned that she was known as the Countess
Prascovie Labinska, a Lithuanian of illustrious
birth and great fortune, whose husband had been
fighting for two years in the Caucasian war.

" It is needless to tell you what diplomacy
I used to be received by the countess, who, in
view of her husband's absence, was necessarily
circumspect in her receptions. At last, however, I was admitted ; two dowager princesses
and four aged baronesses answering for me on
their ancient virtue.

" The Countess Labinska had taken, a mile
or so from Florence, a magnificent villa, a for-

mer belonging of the Salviati family, and in a
short space of time had filled the mediæval
manor with every modern comfort without in
the least disturbing its severe beauty and serious
elegance.   Heavy blazoned portières were in
fit keeping with the vaulted arches from which
they fell; the easy-chairs and other furniture
of quaint and curious shapes harmonized with
the sombre wainscoted walls and the frescoes
dulled and faded to the hues of old tapestry;
and through it all there was not a note that
jarred.   The present did not clash with the
past.   The countess was so naturally the châ-
telaine that the old palace seemed built as her
appropriate setting.

" Fascinated as I had been by the countess'
radiant beauty, at the end of several visits I
was yet more charmed by her brilliant and
subtle mind.   When the conversation was of
interest, her soul shone luminous in her eyes,
the pallor of her cheek glowed with an inner
flame as does a lamp of alabaster : the phosphorescent scintillations, the quivering of light
of which Dante speaks in his description of the
splendors of Paradise, were illustrated in her
appearance, as who should say an angel thrown
in bright relief against a sun.   I stood bewil-
dered, stupefied, and ecstatic.   Lost in contemplation of her beauty, enchanted by the celestial tones of her voice, which made of every

sentence ineffable music, I stammered, when obliged to speak, a few incoherent words, which must have given her a poor idea of my intelligence, and sometimes at certain phrases which denoted on my part either great embarrassment or incurable imbecility an imperceptible smile of friendly irony danced like a rose-colored ripple over her charming lips.

" Still I had not told my love, for in her presence I was without thought, strength, or courage ; only my heart throbbed as would it break its bonds and fling itself at the knees of its sovereign. Twenty times I had determined to explain myself, but an insurmountable timidity restrained me ; the least look of coldness or reserve from the countess threw me into a deathly trance comparable to that of the condemned who, bowed on the block, await the stroke of the axe that is to sever the head from the body. I was strangled by nervous contractions ; I was bathed in an icy perspiration. I reddened, I grew pale, and without having dared to speak I came away, finding the door with difficulty, and staggering down the steps of the house like a drunkard. Once outside I came to my senses, and threw to the wind the most inflamed dithyrambs. I addressed to my absent idol a thousand declarations of an irresistible eloquence. In these mute apostrophes I equaled Love's greatest poets. The

vertiginous perfume of the Orient, the poetry
of Solomon's Song of Songs, hallucinated with
hashish, the platonic subtleties and ethereal
delicacy of Petrarch's sonnets, the nervous and
delirious sensibility of Heine's 'Intermezzo,'
could not compare with the exhaustless effu-
sions of the soul in which my life wasted itself
away. At the end of each monologue it seemed
to me that the countess, vanquished, at last,
must descend from the heavens to my heart,
and frequently I clasped my arms to my bosom,
thinking to enfold her in them.

" I was so completely possessed that I spent
hours in murmuring like a litany of love the
two words, — Prascovie Labinska; and in
these syllables, dropped slowly like pearls, or
repeated with the feverish volubility of a dev-
otee exalted by prayer, I found an indefinable charm. Then again, I wrote the adored
name on the finest parchment, illuminating it
like a mediæval manuscript with flowered designs and traceries of azure and gold. In this
work of pathetic minuteness and puerile perfection I passed the long hours which separated my visits to the countess. I could not
read or otherwise occupy myself. Nothing but
Prascovie interested me, and even my letters
from France lay unopened. I made repeated
efforts to overcome this condition ; I tried to recall the axioms of seduction accepted by young

men, the stratagems used by the Valmonts of
the Café de Paris and the Don Juans of the
Jockey Club ; but to execute them my heart
failed me, and I regretted that I had not, like
Stendhal's Julien Sorel, a package of progres-
sive epistles which I could copy and send to
the countess. Unfortunately, I could only sur-
render myself, without the power to ask a return, without even a hope in the future ; indeed,
in my most audacious dreams I hardly dared
touch with my lips the tips of Prascovie's rosy
fingers. A fifteenth-century novice prostrate
on the steps of an altar, a chevalier kneeling in
his rigid armor, could not have had a more
self-annihilating adoration for the Virgin."

M. Balthazar Cherbonneau had listened to
Octave with profound attention ; for to him the
young man's story was not merely a tale of
romance, and he murmured, during a pause in
the narrative, as if to himself, "Yes, that is
certainly a diagnostic of love, a curious malady which I have encountered but once, — at
Chandernagore, — in a young Pariah in love
with a Brahman ; it killed her, poor girl, but
she was a savage ; you, M. Octave, you are a
civilized being, and we will cure you." This
parenthesis concluded, he motioned M. de Saville to continue ; and, doubling back his leg
to the thigh, like the articulated limb of a
grasshopper, so as to support his chin on his

knee, he settled himself in this position, impossible to any one else, but which to him appeared very restful.

" I do not want to bore you with the details of my secret martyrdom," resumed Octave; " I will hasten to a decisive scene. One day, unable to restrain my imperious desire to see the countess, I went to her before the hour at which she was accustomed to receive. The weather was heavy and overcast. Mme. Labinska was not in the salon. She was seated under a portico, which was supported by graceful columns, and opened on a terrace, from which one descended to the garden; she had had her piano, a wicker lounge, and a few chairs brought out, and jardinières filled with splendid flowers (nowhere are they so fresh and odorous as in Florence) stood between the columns, and impregnated with their perfume the infrequent breezes which came from the Apennines. In front, through the openings of the arcades, one could see the well-pruned yew and box trees, peopled with mythological statues in the labored style of Baccia Bandinelli or of Ammanato, and here and there a tall centenary cypress. In the dim distance rose the dome of Santa Maria del Fiore, and the square belfry of Palazza Vecchio jutted above the silhouette of the town.

" The countess was alone, and reclining

on her lounge; never had I thought her so beautiful; in indolent languor she lay like a water nymph, billowed in the foamy whiteness of an ample India-muslin gown that was bordered with a frothy trimming which resembled the silvery edge of a wave, and clasped at the throat by an exquisitely chased Khorassan brooch. In brief, her costume was as airy as the drapery which floats about the figure of Victory. Her arms, fairer than the alabaster in which Florentine sculptors copy antique statues, issued from wide sleeves open to the shoulder like pistils from a flower chalice; a broad black sash knotted at the waist with falling ends contrasted sharply with all this whiteness; but the melancholy effect which these shades ascribed to mourning might have given was enlivened by the point of a tiny Circassian slipper of blue morocco figured with yellow arabesques, which peeped from beneath her skirt.

"The countess' blonde hair, slightly raised as if by a passing zephyr, revealed her smooth forehead and transparent temples, and formed a nimbus, through which the light glittered in a shower of gold.

"On a chair near by, a large hat of rice straw, trimmed with long black ribbons, similar to those on her dress, fluttered in the breeze, and by it was a pair of unworn gloves of Swedish kid. On my arrival Prascovie closed the

book she was reading, — the poems of Mickiewicz, — and gave me a kindly nod ; she was
alone, a circumstance as uncommon as it was
favorable. I seated myself opposite her on the
chair she designated, and for some minutes one
of those silences fell upon us which are so painful if prolonged. None of the commonplaces
of conversation came to my aid ; my thoughts
were confused, waves of flame rose from my
heart to my eyes, and my passion cried, ' Do
not lose this opportunity.'

"I do not know what I might have done if
the countess, divining the cause of my emotion, had not partly risen, and extended her
beautiful hand as though to close my mouth.

" 'Not a word, Octave. You love me, I
know, I feel, I believe it ; nor does it anger me,
for love is involuntary. Stricter women than
I would be offended, but I pity you because I
cannot return it, and it pains me to be the
cause of your unhappiness. I regret that we
should have met, and blame the whim which
made me leave Venice for Florence. At first
I hoped that my persistent coldness would
weary and estrange you, but nothing rebuffs
true love, of which I see all the signs in your
eyes. Do not let my sympathy arouse in you
either dreams or illusions ; nor must you take
it as an encouragement. An angel with diamond shield and flaming sword protects me

more surely than religion, duty, or virtue against every seduction; and this angel is my love: I adore the Count Labinski. I have had the good fortune to make a love-match.'"

"A flood of tears burst from my eyes at this frank, loyal, yet modest avowal, and I felt the spring of life break within me.

"Prascovie rose in extreme agitation, and, with a motion of gracious feminine pity, pressed her delicate handkerchief to my eyes.

"'There, do not weep,' she said; 'I forbid it. Try to divert your thoughts; imagine that I have forever disappeared, that I am dead; forget me. Travel, work, do good; mingle actively in the tide of life; console yourself with art or love'... At this I interrupted her with a gesture.

"'Do you think,' she asked, 'you would suffer less in continuing to see me? If so, come. I will always receive you. God says we must pardon our enemies; why, then, should we ill-treat those who love us? Nevertheless, absence seems to me a more certain remedy. In two years we can shake hands without danger — for you,' she added, attempting a smile.

"The next day I left Florence; but neither study, travel, nor time has diminished my suffering. I am dying: do not prevent it, doctor!"

"Have you seen the countess since?" asked

the physician, with an odd sparkle in his blue eyes.

"No," answered Octave, "but she is in Paris," and he extended a card on which was engraved :

The Countess Prascovie Labinska. And in a a corner, *Thursdays.*

III.

AMONG the infrequent passers who follow the Avenue Gabriel from the Turkish Embassy to the Elysée Bourbon, and prefer the silence, solitude, and fragrant calm of this avenue to the dusty whirl and noisy elegance of the Champs-Elysées, there are few who would not pause with mingled feelings of admiration and envy before a poetic and mysterious dwelling where for once felicity seemed to be lodged by wealth.

Who is there who has not halted at the railing of a park and gazed attentively through the green foliage at some white villa, and then passed on with heavy heart, as if the dream of his life lay hidden behind the walls? Then, again, other dwellings seen thus from the outside cause an indefinable melancholy. The gray gloom of desertion and despair has settled upon them and blighted the tops of the surrounding trees; the statues are moss-stained, the flowers droop, the water stagnates in the fountain; in spite of the rake, the paths are overrun with weeds, and if there are birds they are dumb.

The gardens on the Avenue Gabriel are separated from the sidewalk by a hedge, and extend in strips of varying size to the houses which face the Faubourg Saint-Honoré. The one alluded to ended at the street in an embankment supporting a wall of rocks chosen for the curious irregularity of their shape. The sides of this wall, being much higher than the centre, formed a rough, dark frame for the radiant landscape set between. The crevices of the rocks held soil enough to nourish the roots of rich plants and flowers, whose variegated verdure was thrown into relief against the sombre hue of the stone. No artist could have created a more effective foreground.

The walls that inclosed the sides of this miniature paradise disappeared under a curtain of climbing plants, of which the stalks, shoots, and tendrils formed a trellis of green. Thanks to this arrangement, the garden resembled an opening in a forest rather than a narrow grassplot shut in the limits of civilization.

Just behind the rock-work stood several groups of slender trees, whose thick foliage contrasted picturesquely. Beyond them spread a plot of turf, without an uneven spear of grass. Finer, softer than the velvet of a queen's mantle, it was of that ideal green rarely obtained, except before the steps of a feudal English manor; a natural carpet on which the eye loves to rest, and the foot fears to crush; an emerald rug where, during the day, the pet gazelle frolics in the sun with the lace-frocked scion of an hundred earls, and where by moonlight a Titania of the West End glides hand in hand with an Oberon inscribed in the peerage. A path of sand, sifted through a sieve that no bit of shell or edge of flint should fret the aristocratic foot, circled like a yellow ribbon around this thick, smooth lawn, which, leveled by the roller, was moistened even in the dryest days of summer with the artificial rain of the sprinkler. At the end of the grass-plot blazed a bed of geraniums, a display of flowery fireworks, whose scarlet stars flamed against a dark mass of heath.

The charming façade of the house closed the perspective. Slim Ionic pillars, and a classical roof surmounted at each corner by graceful marble statues, gave it the appearance of a Greek temple transported by the fancy of a millionnaire, and subdued, by a suggestion of art and poetry, all that might otherwise have seemed ostentatious luxury; between the pillars awnings slashed with crimson were usually lowered, shading and defining the windows which opened, at full length, like glass doors, under the portico.

When the capricious sky of Paris deigned to stretch a bit of blue behind this dainty palace it looked so lovely in its thicket of verdure that it might easily have been taken for the abode of a fairy queen, or for one of Baron's pictures enlarged.

Extending into the garden from each side of the house were two conservatories, whose crystal panes, set in gilt, sparkled in the sun, and gave to a world of the rarest exotic plants the illusion of their native air.

A matutinal poet strolling in the Avenue Gabriel at dawn would have heard the nightingale trilling the last notes of his nocturne, and seen the blackbird in his yellow slippers quite at home in the garden walks. At night, in the silence of the sleeping city, when the roll of carriages returning from the Opéra has ceased, the same poet might have dimly distinguished a white-robed form clinging to the arm of a young and handsome man, and he would certainly have returned to his solitary attic sad and depressed.

The reader, doubtless, divines that here lived the Countess Prascovie Labinska and her husband. Count Olaf Labinski had returned from the Caucasian war after a glorious cam-

paign, in which, if he had not fought face to
face with the mystical and intangible Schamyl,
at least he had attacked the most devout and
fanatic Mourides of the illustrious Sheik. He
avoided bullets as only the brave can, by rush-
ing to meet them, and the curved scimiters o
the warlike barbarians had broken on his chest
without so much as scratching him. Courage
is a flawless cuirass. The Count Labinski
possessed the mad valor of the Slav races, who
love danger for its own sake, and to whom can
be applied the refrain of an old Scandinavian
song : " They kill, die, and laugh ! "

The rapture with which husband and wife,
to whom marriage was a passion sanctioned
by God and man, were reunited could only be
described by Thomas Moore in the style of
the "Loves of the Angels"! To portray it,
each drop of ink would have to be transformed to a drop of light, and each word
evaporate on the paper with the flame and
the perfume of a grain of incense. What picture is possible of souls melted in one like
two dew-drops which, dissolving on a lily petal,
meet, blend, absorb one another, and form but
a single gem?

Happiness is so rare in this world that man
has not thought to invent words to depict it,
while on the other hand the vocabulary of suffering, moral and physical, fills innumerable
columns in the dictionaries of all languages.

Lovers, even in childhood, the hearts of Olaf and Prascovie had never throbbed to other names. In fact, knowing almost from the cradle that they were destined for each other, the rest of the world was but landscape to them. One might have said that they were the twin halves of Plato's Androgyne, which, seeking each other since the primeval divorce, were at last united and joined together. In short, they formed that duality in unity which is known as perfect harmony ; and, side by side, they marched, or rather sped, through life with an equal impulse, sustained and impelled, as Dante has it, "like two doves beckoned by the same desire."

That nothing might disturb this felicity, a colossal fortune enveloped it in an atmosphere of gold. When this radiant couple appeared, Misery, consoled, shed its rags, and dried its tears; for Olaf and Prascovie had the noble egotism of happiness, and could not endure affliction amid their own delight.

Since polytheism has disappeared, and with it the young gods, the smiling genii, the celestial youths whose forms were absolute in perfection, harmonious in rhythm, and perfect in idealism, and since ancient Greece no longer chants the hymn to beauty in Parian strophes, man has cruelly abused his permission to

be ill-favored. Although fashioned in God's
image, he is but a poor likeness of him.

The Count Labinski, however, had not profited by this license. His face was an elon-
gated oval; his nose was clearly and boldly
cut; his mouth firmly outlined and accentuated
by a pointed blonde mustache; his chin, cleft
by a dimple, was ever raised ; while his black
eyes, through a striking and pleasing singularity, caused him to look like one of the warrior
angels, St. Michael or Raphael, who, mailed
in gold, combated the devil. In fact, he would
have been too handsome were it not for the
virile light which shone from the dark iris of
his eyes, and the shade of bronze that the sun
of Asia had spread over his features.

The count was of middle height, slight,
graceful, nervous, concealing, beneath an apparent delicacy, muscles of steel. When for
some embassy ball he donned a magnate's costume, that was embossed with gold, glittered
with diamonds, and embroidered with pearls,
he passed through the throng like a shining
apparition, exciting the jealousy of the men
and the admiration of the women, to whom,
be it said, Prascovie rendered him indifferent.
We need not add that the count was as intelli-
gent as he was handsome ; the good fairies had
visited his cradle, and the evil witch who spoils
everything was in a good humor that day.

It is easy to understand that with such a rival Octave de Saville stood a poor chance, and also, that he was sensible in allowing himself to expire quietly on the cushions of his sofa, and that, too, despite the hope with which the fantastic physician, Balthazar Cherbonneau attempted to revivify his heart. The only way was to forget Prascovie, and that was impossible. To see her was evidently useless. Octave felt that the countess' resolution would never weaken in its gentle implacability and compassionate coldness. He was afraid that in the presence of his innocent and beloved assassin his wounds might reopen and bleed, and he did not wish to accuse her.

IV.

Two years had passed since the day when the Countess Labinska had prevented Octave from making the declaration of love to which she had no right to listen. Awakened from his dream, Octave had taken his departure a prey to the blackest despair, and had not since communicated with her. The one word he would have wished to write was forbidden. Surprised at his silence, the countess' thoughts had frequently and sorrowfully turned to her unfortunate admirer: had he forgotten her? The

simplicity of her nature made her hope that he
had, without being able to believe that he had
really done so, for the light of inextinguishable
passion which blazed in Octave's eyes was not
of a character to be misinterpreted. Love
and the gods are recognized at first sight.
The limpid azure of her content was slightly
clouded by this knowledge, and it inspired her
with the tender melancholy of the angels who,
in heaven, have yet a thought for earth. Her
gentle spirit suffered that she should be the
cause of pain ; but what can the golden star
shining on high do for the obscure shepherd
holding up his mortal arms. In mythological
times it is true Diana descended in silvery
rays upon the sleeping Endymion, but then
Diana was not married to a Polish count.

The Countess Labinska, upon her arrival
in Paris, had sent Octave the commonplace
invitation which Dr. Balthazar Cherbonneau
was twirling abstractedly between his fingers.
Though she had wished him to come and see
her, yet when he failed to do so she said to
herself with a feeling of involuntary joy, "He
loves me still!" She was a woman of angelic
purity, and chaste as the uppermost snow of
the Himalayas ; but God himself in the depth
of the infinite has to distract him from the
monotony of eternity only the pleasure of
hearing the beating heart of some poor, per-

ishable creature on a puny globe that is itself lost in the immensities of space. Prascovie was not sterner than God, and Count Olaf could not have censured this delicate voluptuousness of the soul.

"Your story, to which I have listened attentively," said the physician to Octave, " proves to me that all hope on your part would be chimerical. The countess will never share your love."

"You see, Monsieur Cherbonneau, that I was right in not trying to retain my ebbing life."

"I said," the physician continued, "that ordinary remedies were useless. But, in lands which the stupidity of civilization regards as barbarous there are occult powers, of which contemporary science is absolutely ignorant. In those lands primitive man in his first contact with the vivifying forces of nature acquired a knowledge which is believed to have since been lost, a knowledge which the migrating tribes, the founders of races, were unable to preserve. This knowledge, handed down from initiate to initiate in the dumb recesses of temples, was subsequently confided to hieroglyphics paneled across the walls of the Elloran crypt in sacred idioms, unintelligible to the vulgar. But on the summit of Meru,— the cradle of the Ganges, at the foot of the marble stairs of the holy city of Benares, in depths of the ruined pagodas of Ceylon, aged Brahmans are to be seen deciphering forgotten manuscripts, yogis, who, unconscious of the birds that nest in their hair, pass their lives in repeating the ineffable syllable Om, and fakirs whose shoulders still bear the cicatrices of the Juggernaut's iron stamp. These are the ultimate depositaries of the lost arcana, and it is they who, when they so deign, are able with their esoteric lore to produce the most marvelous effects.

"The materialism of Europe has not the faintest conception of the spirituality which the Hindus have reached : the protracted fasts, the self absorption, the impossible attitudes maintained for years together, attenuate their bodies to such an extent that to see them crouched beneath a molten sun, between glowing braziers, their long nails buried in the palms of their hands, one might fancy they were Egyptian mummies withdrawn from their tombs, and bent double in apelike positions. Their mortal envelope is but a chrysalis, which the immortal butterfly, the soul, can abandon or resume at will. While their meagre form, inert and hideous, lies like a night moth surprised by the dawn, their untrammeled spirit rises on the wings of hallucination through incalculable distances to the spheres of the supernatural. They are visited by dreams and

visions; from one ecstasy to another they follow the undulations that the ages make as they
sink and subside in the oceans of eternity.
To them the infinite delivers up its secrets;
they assist at the creation of worlds, at the
genesis and metamorphosis of gods; they recall the sciences that have been engulfed in
plutonian and diluvian cataclysms, the unre-
membered relations of man and of nature.
When in this condition they mumble words
that no child of earth has lisped for æons; they
intercept the primordial tongue, the Logos
which made light spring from the archaic
shadows. They are regarded as madmen;
they are almost gods ! "

This singular preamble aroused Octave's
attention to the last degree. He was unable
to understand what connection there could be
between his love for the countess and the
mummeries of the Hindus, and, in consequence, his eyes bristled with interrogation
points. His state of mind was divined by the
physician who, waving aside his questions with
a gesture as who should say, Be patient, you
will see in a moment that I am not digressing,
continued as follows : —

" Outwearied of questioning, scalpel in hand,
the dumb corpses in the amphitheatres, corpses
that disclosed but death to me who sought
life, I formed the project, — and one, be it

said, as audacious as that of Prometheus who
scaled the heavens to rob them of fire, — I
formed the project of intercepting and surprising the soul, of analyzing and dissecting it, if
I may so express myself. I passed over the
effect; I looked for the cause ; and therewith
conceived an immense disdain for the self-evi-
dent nothingness of materialism.

" To work over a fortuitous combination of
evanescent molecules seemed to me worthy
only of a vulgar empiric. I attempted to
undo with magnetism the bands that join
mind and matter. In experiments that were
certainly prodigious, but which failed to satisfy
me, I surpassed Mesmer, Deslon, Maxwell,
Puységur, and Deleuze : Catalepsy, somnam-
bulism, clairvoyance, soul projection, in fact,
all the effects which are incomprehensible to
the masses, though simple enough to me, I
produced at will. Nay, I did more ; from the
ecstasies of Cardan and St. Thomas of Aqui-
nas I ascended to the self-abstraction of the
Pythians ; I penetrated the mysteries of the
Greeks ; the arcana of the Hebrews ; I pierced
the innermost wisdom of Trophonius and Æs-
culapius, and therewithal, I found in their now
traditional miracles that by a gesture, a word,
a glance, by mere volition or some other unknown agent, the soul would shrink or expand.
One by one I repeated all the miracles of

Apollonius of Tyana. Yet still my ambition was unfulfilled; the soul escaped me; I could feel it, hear it, act upon it, but between it and myself there was a veil of flesh that I could not draw aside. Did I do so, the soul had vanished. I was like the bird-catcher who holds a bird beneath a net which he dare not raise lest his winged prey shall mount the sky and escape him.

"I went, therefore, to India. In that land of archaic wisdom I hoped to find the solution of the riddle. I learned Sanskrit and Prakrit, the idioms of the erudite, and the language of the people. I enabled myself to converse with Pundits and Brahmans. I crossed the tiger-haunted jungles. I skirted the sacred lakes possessed of crocodiles. I forced my way through impenetrable forests, scattering the bats and monkeys before my path, and at times, in a byway made by savage beasts, I halted abruptly face to face with an elephant. And all this to reach the hut of some far-famed yogi, one in communication with the Mahatmas; and near him I would sit for days sharing his gazelle skin, and noting the vague incantations that fell from his black, cracked lips. In this manner I caught the all-powerful words, the evoking formulas, the syllables of the creating Logos.

" In the interior recesses of pagodas that no

eye save that of the initiate has seen, but which the garb of a Brahman permitted me to penetrate, I studied the symbolic sculptures. I read many of the cosmological mysteries, many of the legends of lost civilizations. I discovered the meaning of the emblems that the hybrid gods, profuse as Indian vegetation, clutch in their multiple hands. I meditated over Brahma's circle, Vishnu's lotus, the cobra de capello of the blue god Siro. Ganesa unrolling her pachyderm trunk, and winking her small eyes fringed with long lashes, seemed to smile at my efforts and encourage my researches. Each one of these monstrous figures appeared to whisper in their language of stone: 'We are but forms; it is the Spirit that stirs.'

" A priest of the Temple of Tirunamalay, to whom I disclosed my intentions, told me of a yogi who dwelt in one of the grottoes of the isle of Elephanta, and who had reached the highest degree of sanctity. I found him propped against the wall of the cavern. Robed in sackcloth, his knees drawn up to his chin, his fingers clasped around his legs, he crouched there motionless. His upturned pupils left visible only the whites of his eyes; his drawn lips exposed his teeth; his skin clung to his cheekbones; his hair, thrown back, hung in stiff locks like overhanging plants; his beard, divided in two floods, nearly touched the ground; and his nails curved inward like an eagle's claw.

" His skin, naturally brown, had been dried and darkened by the sun till it resembled basalt, and, thus seated, he looked, both in form and color, like a Canopic vase. At first I thought him dead. His arms, that were anchylosed in a cataleptic immobility, I shook in vain; in his ear I shouted the most powerful of the sacramental words which were to reveal me to him as initiate, but he heeded them not, nor did his eyelids quiver. In my despair of arousing him I was about to leave him, when suddenly I heard a singular rustle; swift as a lightning flash a bluish spark passed before my eyes, hovered for a second on the half-open lips of the penitent, and disappeared.

" Brahma-Logum (such was the name of this holy personage) seemed to awake from a lethargy; he opened his eyes, gazed at me in a natural manner, and answered my questions. 'Your wish is fulfilled,' he said; 'you have seen a soul. I have succeeded in freeing mine from my body whenever it so pleases me; it goes and returns like a luminous bee, perceptible only to the eyes of the adept. I have fasted, I have prayed, I have meditated so long, I have dominated the flesh so rigorously, that I have been able to loose the terrestrial bonds. Vishnu, the god of the tenfold incarnations, has revealed to me the mysterious syllable that guides the soul in its avatars. If, after making the consecrated gestures, I were to pronounce that word, your soul would fly away and animate whatever man or beast I might designate. I bequeath you this secret, which of the whole world I am now the sole possessor. I am glad you have come, for I long to disappear in the bosom of the Increate as does the drop of water that falls in the sea.' And therewith the penitent whispered in a voice as feeble as the last gasp of the moribund, but very distinctly, a few syllables which made a shudder, such as that which Job has mentioned, run down my back."

" Doctor," cried Octave, " what do you mean? I dare not fathom the awful profundities of your thought."

" I mean," M. Balthazar Cherbonneau tranquilly replied, " that I have not forgotten my friend Brahma-Logum's magic formula, and that the Countess Prascovie will be clever indeed if she recognizes the soul of Octave de Saville in the body of Olaf Labinski."

V.

DR. BALTHAZAR CHERBONNEAU's reputation as physician and wonder-worker had begun to be noised through Paris. His eccentricities, affected or natural, had made him the fashion.

But far from seeking to form what is called a practice, he rebuffed his patients by shutting the door in their faces, giving strange prescriptions, or ordering impossible regimens. The cases that he accepted were those that were hopeless ; a vulgar consumption, a humdrum enterite, or a commonplace typhoid he disdainfully dismissed to the care of his brother practitioners. But on supreme occasions the cures he effected were simply inconceivable. Standing at the bedside, he made magic gestures over a glass of water, and bodies already stiff and cold, prepared even for the coffin, after imbibing a few drops of the liquid recovered the flexibility of life, the colors of health, and sitting up again gazed about them with eyes that had become accustomed to the shadows of the tomb. In consequence, he was known as the resurrectionist, the physician of the dead. But it was not always that he consented to use his powers, and he often refused enormous sums from wealthy invalids. To decide him to undertake a struggle with destruction, he must needs be touched by the grief of some mother imploring the restoration of her only child ; by the despair of some lover whose beloved was at the door of death; or else it was necessary for him to consider the patient as one whose life was valuable to poetry, science, or the progress of humanity. In this way he saved a delicious baby that was being throttled by croup's iron fingers, a charming maiden in the last stages of consumption, a poet in delirium tremens, an inventor attacked by cerebral congestion, and whose discovery would otherwise have been buried with him.

Elsewhere he declined to intervene, alleging that nature should not be interfered with, that certain deaths were necessary, and that in preventing them there was a risk of disturbing something in the order that is universal. You can see, therefore, that M. Balthazar Cherbonneau was the most paradoxical of physicians, and that he had brought with him from India a complete outfit of vagaries. His fame as a magnetizer was, however, even greater than his fame as a physician. In the presence of a select company he had given a séance or two, of which the marvels that were related disturbed every preconceived idea of the possible and the impossible and surpassed the prodigies of Cagliostro.

Dr. Cherbonneau lived on the ground floor of an old mansion in the Rue du Regard. The apartment which he occupied was strung out in the manner peculiar to former times. The high windows opened on a garden that was planted with great black-trunked trees topped with vibrant green. Although it was summer, powerful furnaces puffed from their brazen-grated mouths blasts of hot air that maintained throughout the vast chambers a temperature that exceeded a hundred degrees Fahrenheit, for the physician, accustomed to the incendiary climate of India, shivered beneath our pale sun very much as did that traveler who, returning from the equatorial sources of the Blue Nile, shook with cold in Cairo; as a consequence, Dr. Cherbonneau never left his house save in a closed carriage, and on such occasions he wrapped himself in a coat of Siberian fox, and rested his feet on a foot-warmer filled with boiling water.

His rooms were furnished with low couches covered with stuffs from Malabar, inworked with chimerical elephants and fabulous birds; there were detachable stands, colored and gilded by the Ceylonese with naif barbarity; there were Japanese vases filled with exotic flowers; and on the floor from one end of the apartment to the other was spread one of those funereal carpets sprigged in black and white that the Thugs weave for punishment in prison, and of which the woof seems woven of the hemp from the ropes with which they strangle their victims. And therewith, in the corners, were a few Hindu idols of marble and bronze, the eyes long and almond-shaped, the nose hooped with rings, the lips thick and smiling, necklaced with pearls that descended to the waist, singular and mysterious in their attributes, the legs crossed on supporting pedestals. On the walls hung water-color miniatures by some Calcutta or Lucknow artist representing the Avatars which Vishnu has accomplished: his incarnation in a fish, in a tortoise, in a pig, in a lion with the head of man, in a Brahman dwarf, in Rama, in a hero combating the thousand-armed giant Cartasuciriargunen ; in Krishna, the miraculous child in whom the dreamers see a Hindu Christ; in Buddha, adorer of the great god Mahadeva ; and lastly, representing him asleep in the Milky Way on the five-headed serpent coiled in the form of a supporting dais, and there awaiting the hour when for final incarnation he shall assume the form of that winged white horse which in dropping its hoof upon the universe shall cause the world to cease to be.

In the last room, heated to an even greater degree than the others, M. Balthazar Cherbonneau was seated surrounded by Sanskrit volumes. In these volumes the letters had been made with a stylus on thin tablets of wood, which latter were pierced and strung together on a cord in a way which more closely resembled Venetian blinds than books, at least as European libraries understand them.

In the centre of the room an electric machine, its bottles filled with gold leaf and its

glass plates revolved by cranks, raised its complicated and disquieting silhouette beside a
mesmeric bucket spiked with numberless iron
rods, and in which was plunged a metal lance.
M. Cherbonneau was anything but a charlatan,
and did not need a stage setting ; but, nevertheless, it was difficult to enter this weird retreat
without experiencing a little of the impression
which, in olden times, the alchemic laboratories
must have caused.

Count Olaf Labinski had heard of the miracles realized by the physician, and his half-
credulous curiosity had been aroused. The
Slav races have a natural leaning towards
the marvelous, which the most careful education does not always correct, and, besides, witnesses worthy of belief who had assisted at
these séances told things of them which could
not be credited until seen, no matter how much
confidence one had in the narrator. The count
went, therefore, to call on the thaumaturgist.

When he entered Dr. Balthazar Cherbonneau's apartment he felt as if surrounded by
imperceptible flames ; the blood rushed to his
head and seethed in the veins of his temples.
He was suffocated by the excessive heat, and
the lamps burning with aromatic oils, the huge
Java flowers swaying their chalices like censers,
intoxicated him with their vertiginous emanations and their asphyxiating perfumes. He

staggered a few steps towards M. Cherbonneau, who was squatting on his divan in one of those strange fakir-like postures with which Prince Soltikoff has so picturesquely illustrated his book of Indian travels. One might have said, on seeing the angles formed by his joints beneath the folds of his garments, he was a human spider wrapped in his web, and crouching immovable before his prey. At sight of the count his turquoise pupils lighted up in their orbits, as yellow as the bistre of the liverwort, with a phosphorescent gleam, which as quickly died away, as if covered by a voluntary film.

Understanding Olaf's discomfort, the physician extended his hand towards him, and with two or three passes surrounded him with an atmosphere of spring, creating for him a cool paradise out of infernal heat.

"Do you feel better now?" he asked. "Your lungs, accustomed to the Baltic breezes, still icy from their contact with the perpetual snows of the pole, must pant like the bellows of a forge in this scorching air where, nevertheless, I shiver, I, baked, tempered, and, so to speak, calcinated in the furnaces of the sun."

Count Labinski made a sign to show that he no longer suffered from the high temperature of the apartment.

The physician continued in a good-humored tone, —

"Well, you have heard my tricks of leger-
demain spoken of, and you want a sample of
my skill. Oh, I am cleverer than Comus,
Comte, or Bosco."

"My curiosity is not so frivolous," replied
the count, "and I have too much respect for
one of the princes of science."

"I am not an erudite in the acceptation
given to the word; but, on the other hand, in
studying certain subjects disdained by science
I have mastered some unemployed occult
forces, and I produce effects which appear
miraculous, though they are perfectly natural.
By watching for it, I have sometimes surprised the soul; it has made me confidences
by which I have profited, and repeated words
which I have retained. The spirit is everything; matter exists only in appearance. The
universe is, perhaps, but a dream of God,
or an irradiation of the Logos in space. I
rumple at will the garment of the body; I stop
or quicken life, I remove the senses, I do away
with distance; I rout pain without chloroform,
ether, or other anæsthetic drug. Armed with the
force of my will, that electricity of the intellect,
I vivify or I annihilate. Nothing is opaque to
my eyes; my gaze pierces everything; I discern
the radiations of thought; and I can make them
pass through my invisible prism and reflect
hemselves on the white curtain of my brain as

the solar spectrums are projected on a screen. But all that is trifling beside the prodigies accomplished by certain yogis of India who have arrived at the sublimest height of asceticism. We Europeans are too superficial, too inattentive, too matter of fact, too much in love with our clay-prison, to open windows on the eternal and the infinite. Nevertheless, as you shall judge, I have obtained a few rather strange results."

Whereupon Dr. Balthazar Cherbonneau slid back on a rod the rings of a heavy portière which concealed a sort of alcove situate at the end of the room. By the light of an alcohol flame, which flickered on a bronze tripod, Count Olaf Labinski saw a spectacle, at which, notwithstanding his courage, he shuddered. On a black marble table was a young man, naked to the waist, and immobile as a corpse. Not a drop of blood flowed from his body, which bristled with arrows like that of St. Sebastian. He might have been taken for the colored print of a martyr in which the vermilion tinting of the wounds had been forgotten.

"This eccentric physician," Olaf said to himself, "is perhaps a worshiper of Siva, and has sacrificed a victim to his god."

"Oh, he does not suffer at all; prick him without fear; not a muscle of his face will move," said the physician, drawing the arrows from the body as one takes pins from a cushion.

A few rapid motions of the hands released the patient from the web of emanations which imprisoned him, and he awoke, with an ecstatic smile on his lips, as if from a happy dream. M. Cherbonneau dismissed him with a gesture, and he withdrew by a small door cut in the woodwork with which the alcove was lined.

" I could have cut off a leg or an arm without his perceiving it," said the physician, moving his wrinkles by way of a smile; "I did not do it because as yet I cannot create, and man, in that respect inferior to the lizard, has not a sap sufficiently powerful to remake the members cut from him. But if I do not create, I at least rejuvenate." He raised a veil which covered an aged woman who, lost in a magnetic slumber, was seated in an arm-chair near the marble table. Her features, which might once have been beautiful, were withered, and the ravages of time could be read in the emaciated outlines of her arms, shoulders, and bust. The physician fixed his blue eyes on her with obstinate intensity for several minutes. Gradually the tremulous lines strengthened, the contour of the bust recovered its virginal purity, smooth white flesh filled the hollows of the throat, the cheeks rounded into the peach-like bloom and freshness of youth, the eyes opened sparkling in liquid vivacity, and the mask of age, lifted as by magic, disclosed a lovely young woman.

"Do you think the Fountain of Youth has somewhere poured forth its miraculous waters?" asked the physician of the count, who stood stupefied by this transformation. "I, at least, believe so, for man invents nothing, and each one of his dreams is a divination or a memory. But let us leave this figure, remodeled for an instant by my will, and consult the young girl tranquilly sleeping in this corner. Question her; she knows more than sages and sibyls. You can send her to one of your seven castles in Bohemia, and ask her what your most secret casket incloses; she will tell you, for it needs but a second for her soul to make the journey, which is not so surprising, after all, since electricity travels seventy thousand leagues in that space of time, and electricity is to thought what the cab is to the train. Give her your hand to put yourself in communication with her; you will not have to formulate your question, she will read it in your mind."

The young girl replied to the mental interrogation of the count in a voice as lifeless as that of a spectre.

"In the cedar casket there is a bit of clay on which can be seen the impress of a small foot."

" Has she guessed correctly ? " asked the physician negligently, as though quite sure of the infallibility of his somnambulist.

The count's cheeks grew crimson. In the earliest days of his love he had taken the imprint of one of Prascovie's footsteps from an alley in a park, and he kept it, like a relic, in a box of the most costly workmanship inlaid with silver and enamel, whose microscopic key he wore hung at his neck on a Venetian chain.

M. Balthazar Cherbonneau, who was a well-bred man, seeing the count's embarrassment, did not insist, but led him to a table, on which was set some water that was crystal in its clarity.

" You have, of course, heard of the magic mirror in which Mephistopheles showed Faust the image of Helen ; now, without having a hoof in my silk stocking or plumes in my hat, I am none the less able to entertain you with this innocent phenomenon. Lean over this bowl and think intently of the person you wish to see ; living or dead, far or near, she will come at your call from the end of the world or the depths of history."

The count bent over the bowl. Soon the water grew troubled and took on opalescent tints, as if a drop of essence had been poured into it, and a rainbow-hued ring encircled the edge of the dish framing the picture which already sketched itself beneath the creamy cloud.

The mist faded. Through the now transparent water a young woman was revealed. Her loose gown was of lace, her eyes sea green, her hair wavy and golden. Over the ivory keys of a piano her lovely hands strayed like white butterflies. The picture was so marvelous in its perfection that at sight of it artists might have died of despair. It was Prascovie Labinska, who, unconsciously, obeyed the passionate invocation of the count.

"And now let us pass to something more curious," said the physician, grasping the count's hand and placing it on one of the rods belonging to the mesmeric bucket. Olaf had no sooner touched the metal charged with an overpowering magnetism than he fell stunned to the floor.

Taking him in his arms, the physician lifted him up, laid him on the divan, rang, and said to the servant who appeared at the door, —

"Go find M. Octave de Saville."

VI.

IN a little while the wheels of a carriage resounded in the silent courtyard of the hotel, and almost simultaneously Octave was announced. When M. Cherbonneau showed him the Count Olaf Labinski stretched on a sofa, apparently lifeless, he was stupefied. At first he thought murder had been committed, and was struck dumb with horror ; but, on a closer examination, he noticed that the chest of the sleeper rose and fell with an almost imperceptible respiration.

" There," said the physician, " there is your disguise already prepared. It is a little more difficult to put on than a domino ; but Romeo, in climbing to the balcony at Verona, did not worry at the danger he ran of breaking his neck. He knew that Juliet awaited him in the silence of the night. The Countess Prascovie Labinska is well worth the daughter of the Capulets."

Perplexed by the weirdness of the situation, Octave did not answer. His eyes were fixed on the count, whose head slightly thrown back on a cushion gave him the appearance of one of those effigies of knights which, with their stiff necks resting on a carved marble pillow, lie above their tombs in Gothic cloisters. In spite of himself, this chivalrous figure, of which he was to take possession, smote him with remorse.

The physician mistook Octave's perplexity for hesitation. A vaguely disdainful smile flitted across his lips, and he said, —

"If you are not decided I can awaken the count, who will depart as he came, astonished at my magnetic power. But, think it over; such a chance may never repeat itself. Still, however great my interest in your love may be, however much I desire to make an experiment which has never been attempted in Europe, I dare not hide from you that this exchange of souls is perilous. Question your heart. Will you risk your life in this supreme attempt? The Bible says Love is as strong as death."

"I am ready," Octave replied simply.

"Very good," cried the doctor, rubbing his shrunken, brown hands together with an extraordinary rapidity, as if he wished to strike fire in the manner of savages. "A passion which recoils at nothing pleases me. There are but two things in this world — passion and will. If you are not happy it will not be my fault. Ah, Brahma-Logum, from the depths of the sky of Indra, where the Apsaras surround you with their voluptuous choirs, you shall see if I have forgotten the irresistible formula which you gasped in my ear on abandoning your petrified carcass. Word and gestures, I have retained them all. To work! to work! We shall make in our caldron as strange a mess as the witches of Macbeth, without, however, the sorcery of the North. Take this arm-chair in front of me, and give yourself confidently into my power. Good! eye to eye, hand to hand. Already the charm works. The sense of time and space is lost, consciousness fades, the eyelids fall. The muscles, no longer commanded by the brain, relax; the mind is lulled, and all the delicate threads which hold the soul to the body are untied. Brahma in the golden egg, where he dreamed for ten thousand years, was not farther from external things. Now inundate him with electric currents. bathe him in psychic emanations."

While muttering these disjointed sentences, the physician did not for an instant discontinue his passes. Luminous rays flew from his distended hands and struck his patient on the brow and heart, while around him there gathered slowly a sort of visible atmosphere, phosphorescent like an aureole.

"That is perfect!" exclaimed M. Balthazar Cherbonneau, applauding himself for his success. "Now he is as I want him. But there," he cried, after a pause, as if he read through Octave's skull the last effort of his vanishing personality, "what is it that still resists? What is that mutinous idea which, driven from the circumvolutions of the brain, tries to escape my influence by crouching on the primal monad, in the sphericity of life? But I know how to reach and curb it."

To master this unconscious opposition the physician recharged the magnetic battery of his gaze, and caught the rebel thought between the base of the brain and the insertion of the spinal marrow, the most secret sanctuary, the most mysterious tabernacle of the soul. His triumph was complete.

He next prepared himself with a majestic solemnity for the surprising experiment he was to attempt. Robing himself in a linen gown like a Magi, he washed his hands in perfumed water. He took from different boxes powders, and smeared his brow and cheeks with hierarchic designs. He encircled his arm with the Brahman cord, and read two or three Slokas of the sacred poems, omitting none of the minute rites recommended by the Mahatmas of the isles of Elephanta.

These ceremonies terminated, he threw the doors of the furnaces wide open, and soon the room was filled with an incandescent atmosphere, which would have made tigers swoon in the jungle, cracked the cuirass of mud on the hides of buffaloes, and exploded aloes into bloom.

"The two sparks of divine fire which will now find themselves nude and divested for several seconds of their mortal envelope must not pale or waver in our icy air," said the physician, examining the thermometer, which marked 120 degrees Fahrenheit.

Between the inert bodies Dr. Balthazar Cherbonneau, garmented in white, looked like a priest of one of those sanguinary religions which throw the corpses of men on the altars of their gods. Indeed, he recalled that pontiff of Vitziliputzili, of whom Heine speaks in a ballad, though his intentions were necessarily more pacific.

Presently he approached the motionless count and pronounced the ineffable syllable, which he hastened to repeat to Octave, who lay in a profound slumber. M. Balthazar Cherbonneau's face, which under ordinary circumstances was simply fantastic, now assumed a singular majesty. The extent of the power which he wielded ennobled his irregular features, and if any one had witnessed the sacerdotal gravity with which he accomplished these mysterious rites he would not have recognized in him the Hoffmannesque physician who suggested, while defying the pencil of the caricaturist.

Strange things then came to pass: Octave de Saville and Count Olaf Labinski appeared to be simultaneously agitated by a convulsion of agony; their faces, which were of a deathly pallor, twitched nervously, and a slight froth rose to their lips. Two small blue flames scintillated hesitantly over their heads.

The physician made an imperious gesture,

which seemed to trace the way for them through the air, and the two phosphorescent sparks began to move. They crossed to their new abodes, leaving a trail of light behind them. Octave's soul entered the body of Count Labinski, and the count's soul entered that of Octave. The avatar was accomplished.

A flush of red at the cheek-bones showed that life had reëntered the human clay, which, an instant soulless, would, without the physician's power, have become the prey of the angel of death.

Cherbonneau's blue eyes gleamed with joy at his triumph, and he said to himself, as he strode up and down the room, "I should like to see the most noted physicians do as much, — they who are so proud of mending the human machine when it gets out of order : Hippocrates, Galen, Paracelsus, Van Helmont, Boerhaave, Tronchin, Hahnemann, Rasori, the most insignificant Indian fakir squatting on the steps of a pagoda knows a thousand times more than you ! What matters the body when one can command the spirit ? "

At the end of his sentence Dr. Balthazar Cherbonneau cut several capers of exultation, and danced like the hills in the Sir-Hasirim of Solomon ; but, catching his foot in the hem of his Brahman gown, he almost fell on his nose, a trifling accident, which recalled him to his senses and calmed his excitement.

"Now to awake my sleeping friends," said he, after he had removed the smears of the colored powder with which he had streaked his face, and tossed aside his Brahman costume. Placing himself before the body of Count Labinski, which contained Octave's soul, he made the passes necessary to awaken him from his somnambulistic state, shaking from his fingers at each gesture the electric fluid withdrawn.

After a few minutes Octave-Labinski (hereafter we will so call him for the clearness of the story) rose on his elbow, rubbed his hands across his eyes, and cast around him a look of astonishment, not yet lighted by the consciousness of self. When a finer perception of objects returned to him the first thing he noticed was his own form placed quite away from him on a sofa. He saw himself, not reflected by a mirror, but in reality. He gave a cry, — to his horror, this cry did not resound in his own tone of voice; the exchange of souls having occurred during the magnetic sleep, he had no recollection of it, and felt a strange sense of discomfort. His mind, served by new organs, was like a workman whose habitual tools had been taken away and replaced by others. Psyche, exiled, beat with restless wings the vault of this unfamiliar skull, and lost herself in the mazes of a brain in which still lingered traces of unfamiliar thoughts.

When the physician had sufficiently enjoyed Octave's surprise he said, "Well, how do you like your new habitation? Is your soul at home in the body of this handsome cavalier, hetman, hospodar, magnate, and husband of the most beautiful woman in the world? You no longer mean to let yourself die, as was your intention the first time I saw you in your gloomy apartment of the Rue Saint-Lazare now that the doors of the Labinski mansion are open to you, and you need not fear that Prascovie will close your mouth with her hand, as in the Villa Salviati, when you wish to speak of love. You see now that old Balthazar Cherbonneau, in spite of his hideous face,— which, by the way, he can change when he wants to, — has still rather good recipes in his box of tricks."

"Doctor," replied Octave-Labinski, "you have the power of a god, or at least of a demon."

"Oh, oh, do not fear; there is not the slightest deviltry in this! Your salvation is not in danger. I shall not make you sign a compact with a flourish. Nothing could be simpler than what has happened. The Logos which has created light can surely displace a soul. If men would but hearken to God across time and infinity they would see things even more surprising than that."

"With what gratitude, with what devotion, can I acknowledge this inestimable service?"

"You owe me nothing. You interest me; and to an old Lascar like myself, bronzed by every sun, hardened to every event, an emotion is a rare occurrence. You have revealed love to me, and you know we dreamers, who are more or less alchemists, magicians, and philosophers, all seek the absolute. But get up, move about, and see if your new skin is uncomfortable."

Octave-Labinski obeyed, and took a turn or two about the room. Already he was less awkward; though occupied by another soul, the body of the count retained the impulsion of its ordinary habits, and the new guest confided himself to these physical memories, for it was important for him to have the walk, the air, and the gestures of the former proprietor.

"Had I not myself but just operated the exchange of your souls," Dr. Balthazar Cherbonneau said, laughing, "I should think that nothing unusual had happened during the evening, and I should take you for the true, legitimate, and authentic Lithuanian Count Olaf Labinski, whose real self still sleeps there in the chrysalis which you have disdainfully discarded. But it will soon be midnight; and if you do not want Prascovie to scold you, or accuse you of preferring lansquenet or baccarat to her, you had now better go. You must not begin your married life with a quarrel ; it would be a bad omen. In the mean time, I will busy myself in awakening your former envelope with all the care and respect it deserves."

Recognizing the importance of the physician's suggestion, Octave-Labinski hastened to leave. At the foot of the steps the count's magnificent bay horses snorted with impatience, and in champing their bits had flecked the pavement about them with froth. On Octave's appearance a superb green-garbed groom, of the lost race of heyduques, hurried to the carriage-step, which he lowered with a bang. Octave, who had first turned mechanically towards his modest brougham, installed himself in the splendid vehicle, and said to the chasseur, who flung the order to the coachman, "Home ! " The door was hardly closed when the horses started, and the descendant of Almanzors and Azolans, aided by the large cords, swung himself up behind with a lightness one would not have expected of his immense size.

The distance between the Rue du Regard and the Faubourg Saint-Honoré is not long; it was covered in a few minutes ; and presently the huge portals of the mansion opened and gave way for the carriage, which swept about a large graveled courtyard, and stopped with remarkable precision under a pink-and-white striped awning.

The courtyard was vast. Octave-Labinski took in the details with that rapidity of vision which the mind acquires on certain important occasions. Surrounded with symmetrical buildings, and lighted by bronze lamp-posts of which the gas darted white tongues of flame into crystal lanterns resembling those that in olden times ornamented the Bucentaur, the Labinski mansion looked more like a palace than a mere house. Boxes of orange trees, worthy of the terrace at Versailles, stood at equal distances along the edge of the asphalt, which framed, like a border, the carpet of turf forming the centre.

The transformed lover, on setting his foot on the threshold, was obliged to pause an instant and press his hand to his heart to still its beating. He had, indeed, the body of Count Olaf Labinski, but he possessed only its physical attributes ; all the ideas belonging to the brain had flown with the soul of its first proprietor, — this house, which was henceforth to be his, was strange to him ; he was even ignorant of its interior arrangements. A staircase rose before him ; he followed where it led, determined to attribute to abstraction any mistake he might make. The polished stone steps shone brilliantly, and threw into relief the opulent crimson of the broad strip of velvet carpet, which, held in place by rods of gilded brass, traced the way softly underfoot. Stands, filled with beautiful exotic plants, lined the stair. An immense windowed lantern, suspended by a heavy rope of knotted and tasseled purple silk, flashed golden shimmers over the stucco walls, smooth and white as marble, and threw a flood of light on a reproduction of one of Canova's most celebrated groups, Cupid embracing Psyche.

The landing of the first and only story was paved with mosaics of costly design, and on the walls, hung by silken cords, were four pictures, the work of Paris Bordone, Bonifazzio, Palma the elder, and Paul Veronese, whose architectural and pompous style harmonized with the magnificence of the staircase.

A high baize door, studded with gold nails, opened on the landing. Octave - Labinski pushed it, and found himself in a large antechamber, where drowsed several liveried footmen, who at his approach rose as if on springs, and ranged themselves along the walls with the impassibility of Oriental slaves. He passed on. A white-and-gold drawing-room succeeded the antechamber, but there was no one in it. Octave rang a bell. A maid appeared.

" Can madame receive me ? "

"Her ladyship is undressing, but she will be visible presently."

VII.

LEFT alone with the body of Octave de
Saville, which the soul of Count Olaf Labinski
inhabited, Dr. Balthazar Cherbonneau set
himself to work to bring it back to every-day
life. After a few passes Olaf-de Saville (we
must now unite these two names to designate a double personage) came out of the profound slumber, or rather catalepsy, which had
chained him, like a spectre from Hades, stiff
and motionless, to the sofa. He rose with an
automatic movement, undirected as yet by the
will, and staggered from dizziness. Objects
swayed about him ; the incarnations of Vishnu
on the walls danced a saraband. Dr. Cherbonneau, waving his arms like wings, and
rolling his blue eyes in wrinkled, brown orbits which looked like the rims of spectacles,
appeared to him as the Mahatma of Elephanta.
The weird sights at which he had assisted before falling into the mesmeric trance reacted
on his reason, and he grasped reality slowly.
He resembled a sleeper suddenly awakened
from a nightmare, who mistakes the clothes
scattered over the furniture for vague, human
shapes, and thinks the brass curtain knobs,
shining with the reflection of the night-light,
are the flaming eyes of cyclops.

Little by little this phantasmagoria evaporated, and things resumed their natural aspect; M. Balthazar Cherbonneau was no longer an Indian fakir, but a plain doctor of medicine, who smiled at his patient with commonplace good nature.

"Are you satisfied, sir," he said, in a tone of obsequious humility, in which could be discerned a shade of irony; "are you satisfied with the experiments which I have had the honor to make before you? I dare to hope that you will not much regret your evening, and that you will leave here convinced that all that is told of magnetism is not, as official science affirms, mere fable and jugglery."

Olaf-de Saville nodded assent, and left the apartment accompanied by Dr. Cherbonneau, who made him a low bow at each door.

The brougham drove up, grazing the steps, and the soul of the Countess Labinska's husband, which inhabited Octave de Saville's body, entered it without noticing that neither the livery nor the carriage was his.

The coachman asked where his master wished to go.

"Home," answered Olaf-de Saville, confusedly, astonished at not hearing the voice of the chasseur who usually asked him this question with a most pronounced Hungarian accent. The brougham in which he found him-

self was upholstered with dark-blue damask;
his own coupé was lined with buttercup colored satin, and the count, though surprised,
accepted it all much as one does in a dream
where ordinary objects present themselves under strange aspects without however ceasing to
be recognizable. He felt smaller than usual,
also, it seemed to him he had gone to the physician's in evening dress; yet, without remembrance of having changed his clothes, he saw
that he wore a summer suit of thin material,
which had never formed·part of his wardrobe.
His mind was confused, and his thoughts, so
lucid in the morning, unraveled themselves
laboriously. Attributing this singular state to
the weird scenes of the evening, he thought
no more of it; and leaning his head against
the side of the carriage, he drifted into an
undefined reverie, a vague dreaminess, which
was neither waking nor sleeping.

The sudden halt of the horse, and the coachman's voice shouting "Gate!" recalled him
to himself; he lowered the window, put out
his head, and saw by the light of a lamp an
unfamiliar street, and a house which was not
his own.

"Where the devil have you brought me,
fool?" he cried; "are we in the Faubourg
Saint-Honoré, — Hotel Labinski?"

"Excuse me, sir; I did not understand,"

muttered the coachman, turning his horse in the direction indicated.

During the transit the transformed count asked himself several questions which he was unable to answer. Why had his own carriage left without him, since he had ordered it to wait? Why did he find himself in some one else's. For the moment he fancied that the clearness of his perceptions must be obscured by fever, or perhaps that the thaumaturgistic doctor, to impress his credulity more keenly, had made him inhale in his sleep hashish or some other hallucinating drug, whose illusions would be dispelled by a night's rest.

The carriage reached the Labinski mansion. The Suisse, when summoned, refused to open the door, saying it was not a reception evening, and adding that his master had returned an hour ago, and her ladyship had retired.

"Fool, are you drunk or crazy?" cried Olaf-de Saville, pushing aside the giant who rose colossal from the threshold of the half-open door, like one of those bronze statues which, in Arab tales, defend from wandering knights the entrance to enchanted castles.

"Drunk or crazy yourself, my little gentleman," answered the man, who from his natural crimson turned purple with anger.

"Scoundrel!" roared Olaf-de Saville, "did I not respect myself" —

" Be quiet, or I will break you across my knee and throw the pieces on the sidewalk," replied the giant, opening a hand larger than the huge plaster hand in the glove shop of the Rue Richelieu ; "you must not be ugly with me, my little man, because you have drunk too much champagne."

Olaf-de Saville, exasperated, shoved the Suisse so fiercely that he got by under the porch. Several footmen who were still up ran forward at the noise of the altercation.

"I discharge you, stupid animal, wretch, villain ! You shall not even spend the night in the house. Go, or I will kill you as I would a mad dog. Do not force me to spill the base blood of a lackey."

And the count, dispossessed of his body, with blood-shot eyes, foaming lips, and clinched hands, rushed at the enormous Suisse, who grasped his aggressor's hands in one of his own, and held them almost crushed in the vise of his short, thick fingers, fleshy and knotted like those of a mediæval torturer.

"There now," said the giant, who, good-natured enough in the main, and fearing nothing more from his adversary, simply gave him a shake or two to keep him respectful. "There now, is there any sense in getting into such a state when one is dressed like a man of the world, and then come like a rowdy making a racket at night in respectable houses? One owes a certain consideration to wine, and that which has made you so drunk must be famous, that is why I do not knock you down, and I shall just put you gently out on the sidewalk, where the watchman will pick you up if you continue your uproar. A breath of prison air will sharpen your wits."

"Rascals," cried Olaf-de Saville to the assembled lackeys, "you allow this low varlet to insult your master, the noble Count Labinski!"

At this name the footmen with one accord gave a loud shout; a burst of laughter, Homeric and convulsive, lifted their galloon-covered chests.

"This little gentleman who thinks himself the Count Labinski! ha, ha, ha! the idea is good!"

An icy sweat broke out on Olaf-de Saville's temples. A sharp thought pierced his brain like a dagger, and he felt the marrow freeze in his bones. Was Smarra's knee on his chest, or was this real life? Had his reason foundered in the bottomless sea of magnetism, or was he the plaything of some diabolical machination? Not one of his servants, so trembling, so submissive, so prostrate before him, recognized their master. Had his body been changed as well as his clothing and carriage?

"That you may be very sure of not being the Count Labinski," said one of the most insolent of the group, "look, there he is, aroused by your clamor, descending the steps himself."

The Suisse's captive turned his eyes towards the end of the court, and saw, erect under the awning of the marquise, a slender, graceful young man, with oval face, black eyes, aquiline nose, and slight mustache, a young man who was none other than himself, or else his own ghost modeled by the devil with delusive cunning.

The Suisse dropped the hands which he held imprisoned. The lackeys ranged themselves respectfully against the wall, and with lowered eyes, hanging hands, in an absolute immobility, like pages at the approach of the Sultan, they rendered to this phantom the honors which the real count was denied.

Prascovie's husband, though brave as a Slav, a term which implies everything, felt an unspeakable terror at the approach of this Ménechme, who in mingling with real life and making his double unrecognizable was far more terrible than on the stage. An ancient family legend came to his mind and increased his dread. Each time a Labinski was to die, he was warned by the appearance of a phantom exactly similar to himself. Among north-

ern nations to see one's double, even in a
dream, is always regarded as a fatal omen,
and the intrepid warrior of the Caucasus, at
the aspect of this external vision of his own
self, was seized with an insurmountable superstitious horror.   He who would have plunged
his arm in the mouth of a loaded cannon re-
coiled at sight of himself.

Octave-Labinski advanced toward his former
body, in which the count's indignant soul was
struggling and shivering, and said, in a tone
of cold and haughty politeness, —

" Sir, do not compromise yourself with these
servants.   The Count Labinski, if you wish to
speak to him, is visible from noon until two
o'clock.   The countess receives on Thursdays
those who have had the honor to be presented
to her."

Having uttered these sentences slowly, and
emphasized each syllable, the pseudo - count
quietly withdrew, and the doors closed behind
him.

Olaf-de Saville was put in his carriage unconscious.   When he came to his senses he
was lying on a bed unlike his own in shape,
in a room which he did not remember ever to
have entered.   At his side stood a strange
servant, who raised his head and made him
smell a bottle of salts.   " Do you feel better,
sir ?" Jean asked the count, whom he took
for his master.

" Yes," answered Olaf-de Saville ; " it was nothing but a momentary faintness."

" Shall I leave you, sir, or had I better sit up ? "

" No, leave me ; but, before going, light the candelabra by the mirror."

" You are not afraid, sir, that the light will prevent your sleeping ? "

" Not at all ; besides, I am not yet sleepy."

" I shall not go to bed, sir," said Jean, inwardly alarmed at the count's pallor and drawn features, " and if you need anything I will come at the first sound of the bell."

When Jean, after lighting the candles, had gone, the count hurried to the mirror, and in the clear glass where the scintillations of the lights flickered he saw the face of a young man that was sad and gentle, he saw abundant black hair, eyes of a sombre azure, and pale cheeks covered with a dark, silky beard. In fact, a visage which was not his own, and which gazed at him from the depths of the mirror with an air of surprise. At first he tried to believe that some practical joker was framing his face in the brass and inlaid mother-of-pearl border of the Venetian mirror. He felt behind it ; there was no one.

His hands, which he then examined, were longer, thinner, and more veined than his own. On the fourth finger projected a heavy gold ring with a seal, on which was engraved a coat-of-arms, — a shield divided, gules and silver, surmounted by a baron's crown. This ring had never belonged to the count, who wore one that bore an eagle displayed in sable, and for crest a pearled coronet. He searched his pockets and drew out a small card-case containing visiting cards with the name : "Octave de Saville."

The laughter of the lackeys at the Hotel Labinski, the apparition of his double, the unknown physiognomy substituted for his own reflection in the mirror, all this might possibly be the illusions of a disordered brain; but these different clothes, the ring which he took from his finger, were material, palpable proofs, evidence not to be denied. A complete metamorphosis had taken place in him without his knowledge. A magician, without doubt, a devil perhaps, had stolen from him his form, his nobility, his name, his whole personality, leaving him only his soul without means to manifest it. The fantastic stories of Pierre Schlemil and the Tale of Saint Sylvester's Night came to his mind. But La Motte-Fouqué and Hoffmann's characters had only lost the one his shadow, and the other his reflection, and if this strange loss of a projection which every one possesses inspired vexatious suspicions, at least no one denied that they were themselves.

The count's position was far worse. He could not claim his own title with the body in which he was now imprisoned. In the eyes of the world he would pass for an impudent impostor, or at least for a madman. In this deceitful envelope even his wife would disown him. How could he prove to her his identity? Yet surely there were a thousand familiar events, a thousand intimate details unknown to every one else, which, recalled to Prascovie, would make her recognize her husband's soul in this disguise; but of what use would her recognition be even if he obtained it, against the verdict of the world?

He was really and absolutely dispossessed of his self. And he had another anxiety. Was his transformation limited to the exterior change of figure and features, or did he really inhabit the body of another? In this case, what had been done with his own? Had a lime pit consumed it, or had it become the property of some bold marauder? The double seen at the Hotel Labinski could be a spectre, a vision perhaps, but it might also be a physical being, installed in the skin which that fakir-faced physician had stolen from him with infernal skill.

A frightful idea stung his heart like a viper's fang: "But this fictitious Count Labinski pressed into my shape by the devil's hands, this vampire who is now living in my house, whom my servants obey in spite of me, perhaps at this moment he is setting his cloven hoof on the threshold of that room where I have never entered less agitated than on the first night. And does Prascovie smile and, with a divine blush, lean her charming head on that shoulder marked by the devil's claw, taking for me that lying shell, that ghoul, that hideous son of night and hell? Shall I rush to the house, and setting it on fire, shout amid the flames to Prascovie: 'You are deceived; it is not your beloved Olaf whom you press to your heart! You are about to commit an abominable crime which my despairing soul will still remember when Time is weary of turning his hour-glass!'"

Waves of flame surged through the count's brain. He gave inarticulate cries of rage, gnawed his knuckles, and paced the room like a wild beast. Insanity was about to submerge the dim consciousness of self which remained to him. He ran to Octave's toilet table, filled a basin with water, and plunged his head into an icy bath.

His presence of mind returned. He told himself that the age of magic and sorcery was past; that death alone separated body and soul; that in the centre of Paris a Polish count accredited with several millions at

Rothschilds, related to the best families, the beloved husband of a fashionable woman, and decorated with the Order of Saint-André, could not be juggled with in this way. All this was undoubtedly but a joke, in very bad taste, indeed, but still a joke of M. Balthazar Cherbonneau, a joke which could be explained as naturally as the bugbears of Anne Radcliffe's novels. As he was worn out with fatigue he threw himself on Octave's bed, and fell into a deep sleep, so heavy that it resembled death, and which lasted until Jean, thinking his master awake, came in to lay the letters and newspapers on the table.

VIII.

THE count opened his eyes and cast about him an investigating look. He saw a comfortable but simple bedroom. A carpet, spotted in imitation of a leopard skin, covered the floor, and tapestry curtains, which Jean had just drawn back, hung at the windows and hid the doors; on the walls was a green velvet paper simulating cloth. A clock cut from a block of black marble, with a metal dial, surmounted by the statuette of Diana in oxidized silver reduced by Barbedienne, and accompanied by two antique vases also in silver, decorated the mantel, which was of white marble veined with blue. The Venetian mirror in which the count had discovered the previous evening that he did not possess his usual face, and the portrait of an old lady painted by Flandrin, without doubt Octave's mother, were the only ornaments of this rather sad, sedate chamber.

A divan, an arm-chair near the fireplace, a study table covered with books and papers, furnished the room comfortably, but in no wise recalled the sumptuousness of the Hotel Labinski.

"Will you get up, sir?" said Jean in the careful voice which he had adopted during Octave's illness, as he handed the count the silk shirt, flannel trousers, and Algerian gandoura, which formed his master's morning costume. Though the count revolted at putting on a stranger's clothes, he was obliged to accept those Jean offered him or remain naked ; so he put his feet down on the soft black bearskin rug at the side of the bed.

His toilet was soon finished, and Jean, without appearing to have the least doubt as to the identity of the false Octave de Saville whom he helped to dress, asked him, "At what hour will you breakfast, sir?"

"At the usual hour," replied the count, who had resolved to outwardly accept his incomprehensible transformation so as not to raise obstacles to the steps he intended to take to recover his personality.

Jean left the room, and Olaf-de Saville opened the two letters which had come with the newspapers, hoping to get from them some information. The first contained friendly reproaches, and complained that the old habits of comradeship were interrupted without motive; it was signed with a name unknown to him. The second was from Octave's lawyer, and urged him to come and draw a quarter's income long due him, or at least to designate an investment for this money which was lying unproductive.

" So it seems," the count said to himself, "that the Octave de Saville whose body I occupy much against my will really exists. He is not a fanciful being, a character of Achim Arnim or of Clément Brentano: he has an apartment, friends, a lawyer, an income greater than his wants, in fact everything which constitutes the legal status of a gentleman. Nevertheless, it seems to me I am the Count Olaf Labinski."

A glance in the mirror convinced him that this opinion would be shared by no one; the reflection was the same by the clear daylight as by the uncertain flicker of the candles.

In continuing the domiciliary visit he opened

the drawers of the table : in one he found title deeds of property, two one - thousand franc notes, and fifty louis, which latter he appropriated without scruple for the needs of the campaign which he was about to begin; while in the other drawer he noticed a Russian leather portfolio closed by a patent lock.

Jean entered announcing M. Alfred Humbert, who rushed into the room with the familiarity of an old friend without waiting till the servant returned with his master's answer.

"Good morning, Octave," said the newcomer, a handsome young man with a frank, cordial manner; "what are you up to, what has become of you, are you dead or alive? No one sees you; I write, you do not answer. I should avoid you, but I have no false pride in matters of affection, and I come to see how you are. Good heavens! I cannot let a college friend die of melancholy in the depths of this apartment which is as lugubrious as one of Charles the Fifth's cells in the Yuste Monastery. You imagine you are ill, but you are bored, that is all. I shall force you to distract yourself, and I mean to play the despot and take you to a jolly breakfast in which Gustave Raimbaud buries his bachelor freedom."

Uttering this tirade in a half angry, half humorous tone, he took the count's hand in his and shook it vigorously.

"No," answered Prascovie's husband, entering into the spirit of his part, "I am even more indisposed to-day than usual; I am not in good condition; I should sadden and depress you."

"It is true you are pale and you look tired. I will wait for a more favorable occasion. I am off, for I am late for three dozen oysters and a bottle of Sauterne," said Alfred, going towards the door. "Raimbaud will be sorry not to see you."

This visit increased the count's depression. Jean took him for his master, Alfred for his friend. A last trial awaited him. The door opened, and a lady whose hair was streaked with gray, and who in the most striking manner resembled the portrait on the wall, entered the room, took a seat on the sofa, and said to the count, —

"How are you, my poor Octave? Jean has told me that you came in late yesterday in a state of alarming weakness; do take care of yourself, my dear son, for you know how much I love you notwithstanding the grief caused me by this inexplicable melancholy, the secret of which you have never been willing to confide."

"Fear nothing, mother, it is not serious," replied Olaf-de Saville; "I am much better to-day."

Reassured, Mme. de Saville rose and departed, not wishing to annoy her son, who, she knew, disliked to be long disturbed in his solitude.

"Now I am decidedly Octave de Saville," cried the count when the old lady had gone; "his mother recognizes me, and does not divine a stranger under her son's epidermis. Perhaps I am then forever immured in this envelope. What a curious prison for a soul is the body of another! It is hard though to renounce being the Count Olaf Labinski, to lose his coat-of-arms, his wife, his fortune, and to be reduced to a miserable commonplace existence. Oh! to get out of it I would tear this skin of Nessus which clings to me, and I would return it to its owner in a thousand shreds. Shall I go back to the hotel? No! — I should make a terrible scandal, and the Suisse would throw me out, for I have no strength in this invalid's dressing-gown. I must think, and look about me, for I must know something about the life of this Octave de Saville who is at present myself."

He tried to open the portfolio. Touched by chance the spring yielded, and the count drew from the leather pockets first a number of sheets of paper blackened with fine, close writing, and then a square of vellum. On this an unskilled but faithful hand had drawn, with love's memory and a resemblance not always attained by great artists, a crayon portrait which it was impossible not to recognize at the first glance. It was the Countess Prascovie Labinska !

At this discovery the count was stupefied. A feeling of furious jealousy succeeded his surprise; how did the countess's portrait come to be in the private portfolio of this strange young man? how did he get it? who had made it? who had given it to him? Had the religiously adored Prascovie descended from her sky of love to a vulgar intrigue? What infernal jest incarnated him, the husband, in the body of the lover of this woman, till then believed so pure? After being the husband, he was to be the lover! Sarcastic metamorphosis, a reversal of position sufficient to turn one's brain, he might trick himself, be at the same time Clitandre and Georges Dandin ! All these ideas buzzed tumultuously in his mind; he felt he was losing his reason, and he made a supreme effort of will to regain a little composure. Without hearing Jean announce that breakfast was ready, he continued with nervous trepidation the examination of the mysterious portfolio.

The leaves composed a sort of psychological journal, abandoned and resumed at different intervals. Here are several fragments devoured by the count with anxious curiosity.

"She will never love me, never, never! I have read in her soft eyes the cruel sentence than which Dante could find nothing more severe to inscribe on the bronze gates of the *Cité Dolente:* 'Lose all hope.' What have I done to God to be damned alive? To-morrow, after to-morrow, always, it will be the same. The planets may intercross their orbits, the stars in conjunction may knot, but nothing in my destiny will change. With a word she has dispelled the dream; with a gesture broken the chimera's wings. The fabulous combinations of the impossible offer me no chance; the numbers thrown a million times in fortune's wheel will never come up, — there is no winning number for me!

"Fool that I am! I know that paradise is closed to me, and I sit stupidly on the threshold, with my back against the door which will not open, and I weep silently, without violence, without effort, as if my eyes were living springs. I have not the courage to rise and plunge into the immense desert or into the tumultuous Babel of men.

"When, sometimes, in the night I cannot sleep, I think of Prascovie; if I sleep I dream of her. Oh, how beautiful she was that day in the garden of the Villa Salviati, at Florence! That white dress with the black ribbons, it was charming and funereal! The

white for her, the black for me! Now and
then the ribbons stirred by the breeze formed
a cross on the background of startling white,
an invisible spirit was murmuring the death
mass of my heart.

"Should some surprising catastrophe tiara
my brow with the crown of an emperor or ca-
liph, should the earth bleed for me her veins
of gold, should the diamond mines of Gol-
conda and of Visiapour allow me to dig in
their sparkling galleries, should Byron's lyre
resound under my fingers, should the most perfect works of antique and modern art lend me
their charms, should I discover a new world,
well, for all that I would not be further advanced!

"On what a thread hangs fate! If I had had
the desire to go to Constantinople I should
not have met her; I stay in Florence, I see
her, and I die.

"I should have killed myself, but she
breathes the air in which I live, and perhaps
my covetous lip may seize — oh, ineffable joy!
— a distant emanation of that perfumed
breath. And, besides, my guilty soul would
be assigned to an exile's planet, and I should
lose the chance to make her love me in another life. To be separated there, she in
paradise, I in hell: oh, maddening thought!

"Why must I love precisely the one woman

who cannot love me! Others, called beautiful, who were free, smiled on me with their
tenderest smiles, and seemed to invite an
avowal which did not come. Oh, how happy
is he! What sublimity of former life does
God recompense in him by the magnificent
gift of her love?"

It was unnecessary to read further. The
suspicion which the count had conceived at
sight of Prascovie's portrait had vanished at
the first lines of this sad confession. He understood that the cherished image, recom-
menced a thousand times, had been drawn far
from the model with the tender and indefatigable patience of an unhappy love, and that it
was the madonna of a mystical shrine, before
which kneeled a hopeless adoration.

"But perhaps this Octave has made a compact with the devil to divest me of my body,
and then in my form to profit by Prascovie's
unsuspecting love!"

Though it troubled him strangely, the im-
probability of such a supposition in these modern days made the count soon discard it.   ·

Smiling to himself at his credulity, he ate
the now cold breakfast which Jean had brought,
then dressed, and ordered the carriage. When
it was ready, he had himself driven to Dr.
Balthazar Cherbonneau's, and crossed the
rooms which he had entered the day before as

the Count Olaf Labinski, and from which he had come out saluted by all the world with the name of Octave de Saville. The physician was seated, as usual, on the divan in the farthest room, holding his foot in his hand, and seemingly plunged in a profound meditation.

At the sound of the count's steps he raised his head.

" Ah! it is you, my dear Octave. I was about to go to you, but it is a good sign when the invalid comes to the physician."

"Always Octave! I think I shall go mad with rage," thought the count. Then crossing his arms, he stood in front of the physician, and fastening on him a terrible look, said, —

"You know perfectly, M. Balthazar Cherbonneau, that I am not Octave, but Count Olaf Labinski, and you know it, because last evening, on this very spot you stole my skin by means of your foreign witchcraft."

At these words the doctor gave a shout of laughter, fell back on his cushions, and held his sides to restrain the convulsions of his gayety.

"Moderate this excessive mirth of which you may repent, doctor. I speak seriously."

"So much the worse! that proves that the anæsthesia and the hypochondria for which I have been treating you are turning into insanity. I must change the regimen, that is all."

" I do not know what keeps me from strangling you with my hands, you doctor of the devil," cried the count, advancing towards Cherbonneau.

The physician smiled at the count's menace, and touched him with the end of a little steel rod. Olaf-de Saville received a frightful shock, and thought his arm was broken.

"Oh! we have means to compel invalids when they resist," said Cherbonneau, turning on him the look, cold as a douche, which conquers madmen and subdues the lion. "Go home, take a bath, and this excitement will pass away."

Confused by the electric shock, Olaf-de Saville left Dr. Cherbonneau's, more upset and uncertain than ever. He had himself driven to Passy to consult Dr. B.

To this celebrated physician he said, "I am the prey of a strange hallucination; when I look in the glass my face does not appear to me with its usual features; the objects which surround me are changed; I do not recognize either the walls or the furniture of my room; it seems to me that I am not myself but some one else."

"Under what aspect do you see yourself?" asked the physician; "the delusion may come from the eyes or from the brain."

"I see myself with black hair, dark blue eyes, and a pale face framed by a beard."

" A passport description could not be more
exact : you have neither mental hallucination
nor perverted sight. You are, in fact, just as
you describe."

" Oh, no ! I have really fair hair, black
eyes, tanned skin, and a slight mustache *à
la hongroise.*"

" Here," replied the physician, " begins an
alteration of the mental faculties."

" Nevertheless, doctor, I am not in the least
insane."

" Quite true. It is only sane people who
come to me of themselves. A little fatigue,
some excess in study or pleasure, has caused
this trouble. You are mistaken ; the vision is
real, the idea chimerical : instead of being
fair and seeing yourself dark, you are dark
and think yourself fair."

" Still, I am sure of being Count Olaf Labinski, but since yesterday every one calls me
Octave de Saville."

" That is precisely what I said," answered
the doctor. " You are M. de Saville, and you
imagine yourself to be Count Labinski, whom
I remember to have seen, and who, as you
say, is fair. That explains perfectly why you
see yourself in the mirror with another face ;
this face which is yours does not correspond
with your idea and surprises you. Remember
this, that every one calls you M. de Saville, and

consequently does not share your belief.
Come and spend a fortnight here ; the baths,
the rest, the walks under the large trees, will
dissipate this annoying impression."

The count bowed and promised to come
again. He no longer knew what to think.
He returned to the apartment in the Rue Saint
Lazare, and by chance saw on the table the invitation of the Countess Labinska, which Octave had shown to M. Cherbonneau.

"With this talisman," he cried to himself,
" I can see her to-morrow."

IX.

WHEN the real Count Labinski, chased from
his terrestrial paradise by the false guardian
angel who stood on the threshold, had been
taken to his carriage by the servants, the transformed Octave went back to the little cream-
and-gold salon to wait the countess' leisure.

Leaning against a white marble mantel of
which the hearth was filled with flowers, he saw
himself reflected in the depths of the glass
placed on a gilt - legged console opposite.
Though he was in the secret of his metamorphosis, or, to speak more exactly, of his
transposition, he had some difficulty in per-
suading himself that this image, so different

from his own, was the reflection of his present form, and he could not turn his eyes from the phantom stranger who yet had become himself. He gazed at himself and saw some one else. Involuntarily he looked to see if the Count Olaf were not leaning on the mantel beside him and thus throwing his reflection in the mirror. But he was quite alone. Dr. Cherbonneau had done the thing thoroughly.

After a few minutes, Octave-Labinski ceased to consider the marvelous avatar which had placed his soul in the body of Prascovie's husband; his thoughts took a turn more conformable to his situation. This incredible event, of which the wildest visionary would not in his delirium have dared to dream, had been brought about. He was to find himself in the presence of the beautiful and adored being, and she would not repulse him! The only combination which could unite his happiness with the immaculate virtue of the countess was achieved!

At the approach of this supreme moment his soul underwent the most dreadful agony and anxiety; the timidity of true love made it as weak as were it still in the despised body of Octave de Saville.

The entrance of the maid put an end to his combat with this tumult of thoughts. At sight of her he could not control a nervous start, and the blood surged to his heart when she said, —

"Her ladyship can receive you now, sir."

Octave-Labinski followed the woman, for he was unfamiliar with the different parts of the house and did not wish to betray his ignorance by taking uncertain steps. The maid showed him into a good-sized room; it was a dressing-room ornamented with all the most delicate refinements of luxury. A set of wardrobes in precious wood carved by Knecht and Lienhart, formed a sort of architectural wainscoting, a portico of capricious style, rare elegance, and finished execution. The doors were separated by columns around which heart-shaped leaves of convolvuli and bell-like flowers, cut with infinite skill, twined in ascending spirals. In these wardrobes were kept gowns of velvet and of silk, cashmeres, wraps, laces, cloaks of sable and blue fox, hats of a thousand shapes, and all the belongings of a pretty woman.

Opposite, the same idea was repeated with this difference, that the smooth panels were replaced by mirrors revolving on hinges like the leaves of a screen, so that it was possible to see the face, profile, or back, and to judge of the effect of a bodice or a head-dress. On the third side was a long toilet-table with an alabaster-onyx top, where the silver faucets spouted hot and cold water into huge Japanese bowls set in an open-work rim of the same metal ; Bohemian glass bottles sparkling in the candlelight like diamonds and rubies, contained essences and perfumes.

The walls and ceiling were tufted with Nile green satin, like the inside of a jewel-case. A thick Smyrna rug, with softly blending colors, wadded the floor.

On a green velvet pedestal in the centre of the room was set a large chest of fantastic shape in Khorassan steel, chased, embossed, and engraved with arabesques amplificated enough to make the ornamentation of the Ambassadors' Hall in the Alhambra appear simplicity itself. Oriental art seemed to have done its best in this marvelous work, in which the fairy fingers of the Peris must surely have taken part. It was in this chest that the Countess Prascovie Labinska inclosed her ornaments, jewels fit for a queen, which she wore rarely, thinking, with reason, that they were not worth the place they covered. Her woman's instinct told her that she was too beautiful to need magnificence ! In consequence, they only saw the light on solemn occasions when the hereditary pomp of the ancient Labinski family had to appear in all its splendor. Diamonds never lay more idle.

Near the window, whose ample curtains

hung in heavy folds, the Countess Prascovie Labinska, radiantly fair and beautiful, was seated at a lace-covered dressing-table, before a mirror held toward her by two angels carved by Mlle. de Fauveau with the fragile elegance which characterizes that lady's talent; two candelabra, each with six candles, flooded her with light. An ideally fine Algerian burnous, with blue and white stripes in alternation opaque and transparent, enveloped her like a fleecy cloud; the thin material had slipped from the satiny tissue of the shoulders, and revealed the lines of a throat beside which the snow-white neck of a swan would have appeared gray indeed. The opening of the folds was filled by the laces of a batiste gown, a nocturnal attire without a restraining belt. The countess' hair was undone, and fell behind her in a mass as opulent as the mantle of an empress. The flowing golden locks, from which Venus Aphrodite kneeling in her mother-of-pearl shell wrung the drops when she rose like a flower from the blue Ionian Sea, were not more blonde or luxurious! Blend Titian's amber and Paul Veronese's silver with the golden varnish of Rembrandt, make the sun shine through a topaz, and yet you will not obtain the marvelous tint of her wonderful hair, which seemed to give out light instead of receiving it, and which would have merited more than did

Berenice's to shine, a new constellation, among the ancient planets! Two women were dividing, smoothing, and rolling it in coils carefully arranged that the contact with the pillow should not rumple it.

During this delicate operation the countess balanced on the end of her foot a Turkish slipper of white velvet embroidered with gold, small enough to create jealousy in the hearts of the Sultan's khanouns and odalisques. Now and then, throwing back the silky folds of the burnous, she uncovered her white arm, and with a gently impatient motion pushed aside some stray lock of hair.

Reclining in this indolent posture she recalled the graceful figures in the Greek toilet scenes which decorate antique vases, and of which no artist has since been able to reproduce the pure and correct outlines or the youthful and slender beauty. She was a thousand times more seductive than in the garden of the Villa Salviati at Florence, and had Octave not been already wildly in love with her he would then have infallibly become so; but happily, nothing can be added to the infinite.

At sight of her Octave-Labinski acted as if he had seen the most terrible spectacle; his knees knocked together and almost gave way under him. His mouth grew parched. Distress seized him at the throat like the hand of

a Thug, and flames danced before his eyes.
Her loveliness magnetized him.

Reflecting, however, that this stupid and be-
wildered manner fit for a repulsed lover was
perfectly ridiculous in a husband, no matter
how much in love he might still be with his
wife, he made a courageous effort, and stepped
firmly enough toward the countess.

" Ah! it is you, Olaf! How late you are this
evening!" said the countess without turning,
for her head was held by the long braids which
the maids were twisting. Freeing it from the
folds of the burnous, she offered him one of
her beautiful hands. Octave-Labinski grasped
her soft, flower-like hand, carried it to his lips,
and pressed it with a long, burning kiss, — his
whole soul concentrating itself on the little
spot.

It is impossible to know what sensitiveness
of the epidermis, what instinct of divine modesty, what unconscious intuition of the heart
warned the countess; but a crimson flush
spread swiftly over her face. Her throat and
her arms took on the hue of the snow on the
mountain-tops at the sun's earliest kiss. She
started, and, half angry, half ashamed, slowly
withdrew her hand. Octave's lips had given
her the impression of a hot iron. She quickly
recovered herself, however, and smiled at her
childishness.

"You do not answer me, dear Olaf. Do you know that it is over six hours since I saw you? You neglect me," she added, in a reproachful tone; "formerly you would not have deserted me so for a whole long evening. Did you even think of me?"

"All the time," replied Octave-Labinski.

"Oh, no, not all the time. I know when you think of me even at a distance. This evening, for instance, I was alone, seated at the piano, playing a piece of Weber's to soothe my dullness with music; in the sonorous pulsations of the notes your spirit hovered about me for several minutes; but at the last chord it flew away I know not whither, and did not return. Do not contradict me, I am sure of what I say."

Prascovie in fact was not mistaken. It was the moment when Count Olaf Labinski, at Dr. Cherbonneau's, had leaned over the magical glass of water evoking with all the force of a fixed idea an adored image. From that instant, submerged in the fathomless ocean of a magnetic slumber, the count had been without thought, feeling, or volition.

Having finished the countess' toilet, the maids withdrew. Octave-Labinski remained standing, gazing at Prascovie with a look of passion.

Constrained and oppressed by his expression,

the countess wrapped herself in her burnous like Polymnia in her draperies. Only her head appeared above the blue-and-white folds, uneasy but charming.

No human penetration could divine the mysterious displacement of souls performed by Dr. Cherbonneau by means of the Sannyâsi Brahma-Logum formula; still Prascovie did not recognize in the eyes of Octave-Labinski her husband's usual expression, that look of love, chaste, calm, equal, eternal as the love of angels. This look was kindled by an earthly passion which troubled her and made her blush. She did not understand what it was, but she knew something had happened. A thousand wild suppositions crossed her mind. Was she no longer for Olaf anything but a common woman, desired for her beauty like a courtesan? Had the sublime accord of their souls been broken by some dissonance of which she was ignorant? Did Olaf love another, or had the corruptions of Paris sullied the purity of his heart? She asked herself these questions rapidly without being able to answer them in a satisfactory manner, and she told herself she was foolish, but still she felt afraid. A secret terror invaded her as though she were in the presence of some danger, unknown, but divined by that second sight of the mind which it is always wrong to disobey.

Nervous and agitated, she arose and went toward the door of the bedroom. The pseudo-count accompanied her as Othello leads away Desdemona at each exit in Shakespeare's play, with one arm around her waist; but when she was on the threshold she turned white and cold as a statue, stopped a second, gave a timorous glance at the young man, then entered, closed the door quickly, and shot the bolt.

"Octave's look!" she cried, and sank fainting on a sofa. As her senses came back she said to herself: "But how is it that this look which I have never forgotten shines to-night in Olaf's eyes? Why have I seen its gloomy and despairing flame sparkle in the pupils of my husband? Is Octave dead? Is it his soul which gleamed before me an instant to bid me farewell on leaving this world? Olaf! Olaf! If I was mistaken, if I foolishly yielded to empty fears, you will forgive me; but if I had welcomed you to-night I should have thought I was giving myself to another."

The countess assured herself that the door was well bolted, lighted a pendent lamp, and with a sensation of indefinable anguish like a timid child she hid herself in the bed. Towards morning she fell asleep; but strange and incoherent dreams tormented her restless slumber. Ardent eyes — Octave's eyes — stared at her from a mist, and darted at her forks of fire; while at the foot of her bed crouched a black and wrinkled figure, muttering syllables in an unknown tongue. Count Olaf also appeared in this absurd dream, but clothed in a form which was not his own.

We will not attempt to portray Octave's disappointment when he found himself facing a closed door and heard the bolt grating inside. His supreme hope had failed. He had had recourse to strange and terrible methods; he had surrendered himself to a magician, perhaps a demon, risking his life in this world, and his soul in the next, to conquer a woman who escaped him, though rendered defenseless by the sorcery of India. Repulsed as a lover, he was not more fortunate as a husband; Prascovie's invincible purity thwarted the most infernal plots. On the door-sill of the bedchamber she had seemed to him like one of Swedenborg's white angels anathematizing the Evil Spirit.

He could not stay all night in this ridiculous position, so he looked for the count's apartment. At the end of a suite of rooms he found one which contained an ebony columned bed with tapestry curtains, where amid the scrolls and flowers was embroidered a coat-of-arms. The panoplies of Oriental armor, knights' cuirasses and helmets, touched by the reflection of a lamp, threw vague glimmers into the shadow. Bohemian leather stamped with gold gleamed on the walls. Three or four huge carved arm-chairs and a heavy cabinet loaded with ornaments completed this mediæval furniture, which would not have been out of place in the great hall of a Gothic manor. On the count's part this was not a frivolous imitation of the fashion, but a hallowed memory. The room exactly reproduced the one he had inhabited at his mother's, and though often laughed at about it, — this fifth-act scenery, — he had always refused to change its style.

Octave-Labinski, exhausted with fatigue and emotion, flung himself on the bed and fell asleep, cursing Dr. Balthazar Cherbonneau.

Fortunately, the morning brought with it serener thoughts; he promised himself to act hereafter in a more moderate fashion, to dull his glances, and to assume the manners of a husband. Aided by the count's valet, he dressed himself in a plain and simple costume, and went quietly down to the dining-room to breakfast with the countess.

X.

OCTAVE-LABINSKI walked in the footsteps of the valet, for in this house of which he was the apparent master he did not know where the

dining-room was.   It was a vast room on the
ground floor, opening on the court, and in its
noble and severe style recalled both an abbey
and a manor.   Dark oak wainscoting, arranged
in symmetrical designs, reached to the ceiling,
where plaster moulded in relief formed hex-
agonal panels painted blue and delicately ara-
besqued in gold.   On the long panels of the
wood-work Philippe Rousseau had painted the
four seasons symbolically, not in mythological figures, but by trophies of still-life composed of the fruits appropriate to each season
of the year.   Game by Jadin corresponded to
the fruits of Rousseau, and above each paint-
ing gleamed like the disk of a shield an immense plate by Bernard Palissy or Léonard
de Limoges, of Japanese porcelain, Majolica or
Arabian pottery, the glaze opalescent with all
the colors of the prism.   Stags' antlers and
aurochs' horns alternated with the faience, and
at each end of the room rose a large side-
board, as high as the altar-pieces in Spanish
churches, of elaborate architecture and carved
decoration, and rivaling the most beautiful
works of Berruguete, Cornejo Duque, and
Verbruggen.   On their shelves glittered in
confusion the antique silver of the Labinski
family.   Pitchers with fantastic handles, salt-
cellars of ancient shape, large bowls, drinking-
cups, centre pieces shaped by the quaint Ger-

man fancy, all worthy of a place amid the treasures of the Dresden Green Vault. Opposite the antique plate shone the marvelous products of modern silverware. The masterpieces of Wagner, Duponchel, Rudolphi, and Froment-Meurice ; enameled tea-sets with figures by Feuchère and Vechte ; chased salvers, champagne coolers with vine-leaved handles, and bacchanals in bas-relief, chafing-dishes as graceful as the Pompeian tripods, not to mention the Bohemian crystal, the Venetian glass, and the services in old Saxe and old Sèvres.

Oak chairs covered with green morocco were ranged along the walls, and over a table of which the feet were carved like eagle's claws there fell a clear, equal light through the ground white glass set in the centre panel of the ceiling. A transparent wreath of vine-leaves framed this milky square with green foliage. On the table, set in Russian fashion, the fruit was already placed, surrounded by a garland of violets; and under silver covers that were polished like emirs' helmets, the viands awaited the knife and fork. A Moscow samovar hissed forth a jet of steam; and two footmen in knee-breeches and white cravats stood silent and immovable behind the two arm-chairs, facing each other like domestic statues.

Octave, in order not to be involuntarily preoccupied by the novelty of objects with which

he ought to have been familiar, took in all these
things at a glance.

A rustle on the marble slabs, a murmur of
silk, made him turn his head. It was the
Countess Prascovie Labinska who approached
and seated herself, after making him an amica‧
ble little gesture. She wore a morning gown
of pale green and white plaid silk trimmed
with a pinked ruching of the same material.
Her hair lay in thick waves on her temples,
and was gathered at the nape of her neck in a
golden coil resembling the scroll of an Ionian
pillar, a style as simple as it was dignified, and
which a Greek sculptor could not have wished
to change. Her rose-tinted cheeks were delicately blanched by the evening's emotion and
the agitated sleep of the night. An imperceptible aureole of shadow encircled her eyes,
usually so clear and calm. She had a weary,
languid air; but thus softened, her beauty was
only the more penetrating; it acquired a
human touch, the goddess became a woman,
the angel, folding her wings, ceased to soar.

Octave, grown prudent, veiled the flame in
his eyes with a look of indifference.

The countess, with a slight motion of the
shoulders as if chilled by a remnant of fever,
stretched out her small bronze-slippered foot
to the silky wool of a rug that had been placed
under the table to neutralize the cold contact

of the mosaic of white and Veronese variegated marble which paved the dining-room. Fixing her blue eyes on her companion, whom she took for her husband, for with the daylight had vanished the presentiments, the fears, and the phantoms of the night, she spoke a sentence in Polish in a tender, melodious voice, rich with chaste caresses. In moments of affection and intimacy she often used the dear maternal language with the count, especially in the presence of French servants to whom this idiom was unfamiliar.

The Parisian Octave was well up in Latin, Italian, Spanish, and knew a few words of English; but, like all Gallo-Romans, he was entirely ignorant of the Slavic tongues. The bristling bastion of consonants which protects the rare vowels in Polish would have inhibited his access even had he wished to approach it. In Florence the countess had always spoken to him in French or Italian, and the idea of learning the language in which Mickiewicz has almost equaled Byron had not occurred to him. It is impossible to think of everything.

On hearing this phrase, there took place in the count's brain, inhabited by the mind of Octave, a very singular phenomenon. The sounds, so strange to the Parisian, following the folds of a Slav ear reached the usual place where Olaf's mind received and transferred

them into thoughts, and evoked there a sort
of physical remembrance.' Octave had a confused idea of their meaning; words hidden in
the cerebral circumvolutions, in the secret recesses of memory, arose buzzing, ready to reply; but these vague reminiscences, failing to
communicate with the mind, soon dispersed,
and all was again a blank. The poor lover's
embarrassment was dreadful; in taking the
form of Count Olaf Labinski, he had not
dreamed of this complication, and he realized
that in seizing his position he had exposed
himself to severe disasters.

Astonished at Octave's silence, and fancying
that through some momentary abstraction he
had not heard her, Prascovie repeated her remark slowly and in a louder tone.

If he heard more plainly the sound of the
words, the pseudo-count understood their sig-
nification none the better. He made desperate efforts to guess what it might be about,
but for those who do not know them the dense
languages of the North have no transparency,
and if a Frenchman can surmise what an Italian says, he is deaf when listening to a Pole.
In spite of himself, a violent blush covered his
cheeks, he bit his lips, and to keep himself in
countenance hacked furiously at the meat on
his plate.

"One would certainly suppose, my sweet

prince," said the countess this time in French, "that you do not hear, or that you do not understand me."

"Really," faltered Octave-Labinski, hardly knowing what he said, "that terrible language is so difficult!"

"Difficult! Yes! perhaps it is for strangers; but for those who have stammered it at their mother's knee it springs from the lips like the breath of life, and with the unconsciousness of thought."

"Yes, doubtless; but there are times when it seems to me as if I no longer know it."

"What are you saying, Olaf? What! you have forgotten the language of your ancestors, the language of the Fatherland, the language which enables you to recognize your brothers among men, and," added she in a lower voice, "the language in which you first told me you loved me!"

"The habit of using another tongue" . . . ventured Octave-Labinski, at the end of his arguments.

"Olaf," answered the countess reproachfully, "I see that Paris has spoiled you; I was right in not wishing to come here. Who could have told me that when the noble Count Labinski returned to his domains he would no longer know how to reply to the felicitations of his vassals?"

Prascovie's charming countenance assumed a doleful expression ; for the first time sadness cast its shadow on her angelically smooth brow. This strange forgetfulness wounded her inmost soul, and seemed almost treasonable.

The rest of the breakfast passed in silence. Prascovie frowned on the man whom she thought the count. Octave was in torment, for he dreaded other questions which he would be compelled to leave unanswered. At last the countess rose and returned to her rooms.

Left alone, Octave played with the handle of a knife which he was tempted to thrust in his heart, for his situation was unbearable. He had counted on a surprise, and now he found himself involved in the to him issueless labyrinths of an unknown existence. In assuming the body of Count Olaf Labinski he should also have taken from him his previous ideas, the languages he knew, his childhood's memories, the thousand intimate details which compose a man's self, the links binding his existence to the existences of others. But for that, all Dr. Balthazar Cherbonneau's knowledge would not have sufficed. What a fate ! actually to be in this paradise whose threshold he had hardly dared glance at from afar, to live under the same roof with Prascovie, see her, speak to her, kiss her hand with the very lips of her husband, and yet be

unable to deceive her divine modesty, and to betray himself every instant by some inexplicable
stupidity! "It was written above that Prascovie would never love me! And yet I have
made the greatest sacrifice to which mortal
pride can descend; I have renounced my *self*,
I have consented to profit under a strange form
by caresses destined for another!"

At this point in his monologue a groom
bowed before him and asked, with every sign
of the deepest respect, what horse he would
ride. Seeing that the count did not answer,
the man, much frightened at his own bold-
ness, risked murmuring, —

"Vultur or Rustem? they have not been
out for a week."

"Rustem," replied Octave-Labinski, as he
would have said Vultur had not the last name
clung to his distraught mind.

He dressed for riding and started for the
Bois de Boulogne, wishing to give his shaken
nerves a bath of fresh air.

Rustem, a magnificent animal of the Nedji
race, that carried on his breast, in an Oriental
bag of gold-embroidered velvet, titles to a nobility extending back to the first years of the
hegira, did not need to be roused. He seemed
to understand his rider's thoughts, and as soon
as he had left the pavements and struck the
bridle-paths he started off, fleet as an arrow,

before Octave had touched him with the spur. After two hours of hard riding the horseman and his beast returned to the hotel, the one quite calm, and the other fuming, with scarlet nostrils.

The pseudo-count joined the countess, whom he found in her drawing-room, dressed in a gown of white silk flounced to the waist, a knot of ribbon in her hair.

It was Thursday, the day on which she remained at home and received her visitors.

"Well," she said to him, with a gracious smile, for her beautiful lips could not pout for long, "have you regained your memory galloping in the alleys of the Bois?"

"No, my dear," replied Octave-Labinski, "but I have a confession to make."

"Do I not know in advance all your thoughts? Are we no longer transparent to each other?"

"Yesterday I went to see the physician who is so much talked about."

"Yes, Dr. Balthazar Cherbonneau, who made a long stay in India, and has, they say, learned from the Brahmans a lot of secrets, each more marvelous than the other. You even wished to take me, but I am not curious; for I know you love me, and that knowledge is all I require."

"He made such singular experiments before

me, he produced such miraculous effects, that
my mind is still disturbed by them. This eccentric fellow, who has an irresistible power at
his disposal, threw me into a magnetic sleep
so profound that on awakening I no longer
had the same faculties. I had lost the remembrance of many things. The past floated in
a mist of obscurity; my love for you alone
remained intact."

" You were wrong, Olaf, to put yourself under the influence of this physician. God, who
has created the soul, has the right to touch it,"
said the countess in a grave tone; "but man
in attempting to do so commits an impious
action. I hope that you will not go back there,
and I hope, too, that when I say something
agreeable to you — in Polish — you will understand me as you once did."

During his ride Octave had conceived this
excuse of magnetism to palliate the errors which
he could not fail to make in his new life. But
his troubles were not ended. A servant opening the door announced a visitor.

" M. Octave de Saville."

Though he might have expected this meeting
one day or another, at these simple words the
real Octave trembled as if the trumpet of the
last judgment had suddenly sounded in his ear.
He had need to call up all his courage, and
to tell himself that he had the best of the sit-

uation, to prevent himself from reeling. Instinctively he clutched the back of a chair, and thus managed to stand apparently firm and tranquil.

Count Olaf, clothed in the form of Octave, advanced towards the countess with a deep bow.

"The Count Labinski . . . M. Octave de Saville," said the countess, presenting the gentlemen.

The two men bowed coldly, and over the marble mask of worldly politeness which sometimes covers such evil passions shot savage glances at each other.

"You have grown formal since Florence days, Monsieur Octave," said the countess in a familiar and friendly tone, "and I was afraid I should leave Paris without seeing you. You were more assiduous at the Villa Salviati, and you were numbered among the faithful."

"Madam," the pseudo-Octave answered constrainedly, "I have traveled, I have been ailing, ill even, and on receiving your gracious invitation I asked myself whether I should profit by it, for one must not be an egotist and abuse the indulgence that people are good enough to have for a bore."

"Bored perhaps, but never a bore," replied the countess. "You have always been melancholy; yet does not one of your poets say of melancholy,

'After idleness, 't is the best of ills'?"

" It is a report which happy people spread to dispense themselves from pitying those who suffer," said Olaf-de Saville.

As if to beg his pardon for the love with which she had involuntarily inspired him, the countess cast a look of ineffable sweetness on the count, shut up in Octave's body.

" You think me more frivolous than I am ; all real pain has my pity, and if I cannot relieve, I can at least commiserate. I would like to have had you happy, dear Monsieur Octave ; but why have you immured yourself in sadness, why have you refused the life which came to you with its joys, its seductions, and its duties ? Why have you refused my proffered friendship ? "

These simple and sincere phrases impressed the two listeners differently. Octave heard in them the confirmation of the judgment pronounced in the Salviati garden by this perfect mouth unsoiled by lies ; and Olaf, a proof of his wife's unalterable virtue, which nothing but diabolical cunning could overcome. And a sudden madness seized him on seeing his spectre animated by another soul installed in his own house. He sprang at the throat of the false count.

" Thief, brigand, rogue, give me back my body ! "

At this most extraordinary action the countess rushed to the bell and the footmen carried out the count.

"That poor Octave has gone crazy!" said Prascovie while Olaf, struggling vainly, was being taken away.

"Yes," answered the real Octave, "crazy with love! Countess, you are decidedly too beautiful!"

XI.

Two hours after this scene the false count received from the real one a letter bearing the seal of Octave de Saville, — the unhappy dispossessed Olaf had no other at his disposal. It produced an odd effect on the usurper of Count Labinski's body to open a missive sealed with his own crest, but everything had to be peculiar in this abnormal position.

The letter contained the following lines, traced by a stiff hand, in a writing which looked like counterfeit, for Olaf was not accustomed to holding a pen with Octave's fingers : —

"Read by another than yourself, this letter would appear to be dated from a lunatic asylum, but you will understand it. An inexplicable combination of circumstances never before produced, perhaps, since the earth has turned about the sun forces me to act as no man has ever done. I write to myself and put on the address a name which is my own, a name which with my person you have stolen from me. I am ignorant of the plot of which I am the victim and of the circle of infernal illusions into which I have put my foot. You, of course, know all about it.

" If you are not a coward, the mouth of my pistol or the point of my sword will demand of you this secret on a ground where every man, honorable or infamous, answers the questions put to him. To-morrow one of us must have ceased to see the light of day. The universe is now too narrow for us both. I will kill my body filled with your lying spirit, or you will kill yours, wherein my soul rages at being imprisoned.

" Do not try to prove me crazy. I shall have the strength to be reasonable, and everywhere I meet you I will insult you with the politeness of a gentleman and the coolness of a diplomat. The Count Olaf Labinski's mustache may displease M. Octave de Saville, and, every day, feet are trodden on at the exit of the Opéra. I trust that my words, though obscure, will have no ambiguity for you, and that my seconds will come to a perfect understanding with yours as to the hour, the place, and the conditions of the duel."

This letter threw Octave into a quandary.
He could not refuse the count's challenge, and
yet it went against him to fight with himself, for
he had kept a sort of tenderness for his old
envelope. The idea of being forced into this
duel by some open insult made him decide to
accept it, though if necessary he could have
put his adversary into a lunatic's strait-jacket
and thus stayed his arm;. but his delicacy revolted at such a method. If carried along by
an overpowering passion he had committed a
reprehensible action and hidden the lover under the disguise of the husband to triumph
over a virtue above all seduction, he was still
a man not without honor and courage. Beside,
he had not taken this extreme step until, after
three years of struggle and suffering, the moment had arrived when his life, consumed by
love, was escaping him. He did not know the
count; he was not his friend, he owed him
nothing, and he had profited by the hazard-
ous means which Dr. Balthazar Cherbonneau
had offered to him.

Where find seconds? Of course among the
count's friends ; but Octave in the one day he
had lived in the house had had no chance to
meet them.

On the mantelpiece were two vases of china
with gold dragons for handles. One held
rings, pins, seals, and other trifling jewels, —

the other, visiting cards, on which, under the coronet of duke, marquis, or count, were inscribed by skilled engravers in Gothic, round, or English type a multitude of names, Polish, Russian, Hungarian, German, Italian, Spanish, and attesting the roving existence of the count, who had friends in every land.

Octave took two hap-hazard : Count Zamoieczki and the Marquis de Sepulveda. He ordered the carriage, and drove to their addresses. He found them both in. They did not appear surprised at the request of the man whom they thought Count Olaf Labinski. Totally devoid of the sensitiveness of middle-class seconds, they did not ask if the affair could be compromised, and like the perfect gentlemen they were maintained a silence full of good taste as to the motive of the quarrel.

On his side, the real count, or, if you like it better, the pseudo-Octave, was a prey to a similar embarrassment. He remembered Alfred Humbert and Gustave Raimbaud, whose breakfast he had refused to attend, and he requested them to help him in this encounter. The two young men showed considerable surprise at finding their friend involved in a duel, for he had hardly left his room in a year, and they knew his character was more pacific than quarrelsome. But when he had told them that it was a mortal combat, they made no

further objections, and went to the Hotel Labinski.

The conditions were soon arranged. The
adversaries having declared that sword or pistol suited them equally well, a gold coin thrown
in the air decided the weapon. They were to
meet in the Avenue des Poteaux of the Bois
de Boulogne, near the rustic thatched summer-
house, where the fine gravel offers a favorable
arena for this sort of combat.

When all was settled it was nearly midnight,
and Octave went to the door of Prascovie's
apartment. As on the previous evening it
was bolted, and the countess' mocking voice
flung this sarcasm at him through the door, —

"Come back when you know Polish; I am
too patriotic to receive a foreigner."

Notified by Octave, Dr. Cherbonneau came
in the morning, carrying a case of surgical
instruments and a roll of bandages. They
entered a carriage together, MM. Zamoieczki
and de Sepulveda following in their coupé.

"Well, my dear Octave," said the physician;
"so the adventure is already turning into trag-
edy? I ought to have let the count sleep in
your body on my divan for a week. I have
prolonged magnetic slumbers beyond that
limit. But even when one has learned wisdom from the Brahmans, the Pandit, and the
Sanniasys of India, one always forgets some-

thing, and imperfections are found in the best combined plans. But how did Countess Prascovie welcome her Florence lover thus disguised ? "

" I think," replied Octave, " that either she recognized me notwithstanding my metamorphosis, or else her guardian angel whispered in her ear to distrust me. I found her as chaste, as cold, as pure, as polar snow. Doubtless her exquisite nature divined a stranger under the beloved form of her husband. I told you truly that you could do nothing for me; indeed I am even more unhappy than when you paid me your first visit."

"Who can fix a boundary to the soul's power," said Dr. Balthazar Cherbonneau thoughtfully, " especially when it is weakened by no earthly preoccupation, soiled by no human tie, and keeps itself in the glow and contemplation of love just as it left the Creator's hands? Yes, you are right; she recognized you, her heavenly modesty shrank at the look of desire, and instinctively veiled itself with its white wings. I pity you, my poor Octave! Your wound is indeed immedicable. Were we in the Middle Ages, I should say, Get thee to a monastery."

" I have often thought of it," replied Octave.

Presently they reached the meeting ground. The counterfeit Octave's brougham was already at the place designated.

At this early hour the Bois presented a really picturesque aspect, which later in the day fashion makes it lose. Summer was at that stage when the sun has not yet had time to darken the green of the foliage; fresh, translucent tints, washed by the night's dew, variegated the forest, and gave out an odor of tender vegetation. At this spot the trees are particularly fine; perhaps because they have encountered a more favorable soil, or because they are the only survivors of some old plantation. Their vigorous trunks, stained with moss or glossed with a silvery bark, clutch the earth with gnarled roots, and project oddly bent branches. They might have served as models for the studies of artists and decorators who go much further to seek less remarkable ones. A few birds, which later the day's noises silence, chirped gayly in the leafy retreat; a timid rabbit crossed the gravel of the alley in three bounds and ran to hide in the grass, frightened at the sound of the wheels.

These poems of nature surprised in undress occupied the two adversaries and their seconds very little, as you can imagine. The sight of Dr. Balthazar Cherbonneau made a disagreeable impression on Count Olaf Labinski, but he recovered himself quickly.

The swords were measured, their places assigned to the combatants, who after taking off their coats fell into position.

"Ready!" the seconds cried.

In every duel, no matter what the fury of the adversaries may be, there is a moment of solemn immobility: each combatant silently studies his enemy and makes his plan, reflecting on the attack and preparing to parry and thrust. Then the swords seek, provoke, and feel each other, so to speak, without separating; that lasts several seconds, which seem minutes, hours, to the anxiety of the assistants.

The conditions of this duel, apparently commonplace to the spectators, were so abnormal for the combatants that they remained thus on guard longer than is customary. Each had in front of him his own body, and must drive the steel into flesh which had belonged to himself two days before.

The fight was complicated by a sort of unforeseen suicide, and, though both were brave, yet Octave and the count felt an instinctive horror at standing, sword in hand, face to face with their own phantoms, and ready to fall on themselves. The impatient seconds were about to cry again, "Gentlemen, are you ready!" when at last the blades crossed.

Several attacks were parried with agility on each side.

Thanks to his military education, the count was a skillful fencer; he had pinked the plastron of the most famous masters. But if he still had the method he no longer possessed the muscular arm which had routed the Mourides of Schamyl; it was Octave's weak wrist which wielded his sword.

Octave on the contrary felt, in the count's body, an unaccustomed strength, and though less expert, he always parried the steel which sought his breast.

It was in vain that Olaf strove to touch his adversary and risked thrusts which exposed himself. Octave, cooler and more steady, baffled every feint.

The count began to get excited, and his play grew nervous and uneven. Though he would then have to remain Octave de Saville, he wanted to kill this deceptive body which might even deceive Prascovie — a thought which lashed him into an inexpressible rage.

At the risk of being run through, he tried a straight thrust to reach, through his own body, the life and heart of his rival; but Octave's sword wound round his with such a quick, sharp, irresistible movement that the steel was wrenched from his hand, and springing in the air fell several steps away.

Olaf's life was at Octave's disposal; he had only to thrust and run him through.

The count's face quivered; not that he feared death, but he thought that he was about to leave his wife to this body-thief whom nothing hereafter could unmask.

Far from profiting by his advantage, Octave threw down his sword, and motioning to the seconds not to interfere walked towards the stupefied count, whom he took by the arm and dragged into the depth of the wood.

"What do you want with me?" said the count. "Why not kill me when you have the chance? Why not continue the duel after letting me recover my sword if it revolts you to strike an unarmed man? You know that the sun should not cast the shadows of both of us on the ground, and that the earth must receive one or the other."

"Listen to me patiently," replied Octave. "Your happiness is in my hands. I can keep forever this body in which I dwell to-day and which in legitimate propriety belongs to you. It suits me to acknowledge this now that there are no witnesses near us, and only the wild birds, who never repeat, can hear. Count Olaf Labinski, whom I represent as well as I can, is a better fencer than Octave de Saville, whose form you now have, and which I, much to my regret, would be obliged to suppress. This death, though not real, as my soul would survive, would desolate my mother."

Recognizing the truth of these remarks, the count maintained an acquiescent silence.

" If I should oppose it," continued Octave, "you would never succeed in reintegrating your identity; you see in what your two attempts ended. Other trials would stamp you as a monomaniac. No one would believe a word of your allegations, and, as you have already been able to convince yourself, when you pretended to be Count Olaf Labinski every one would laugh in your face. You would be shut up, and you would pass the rest of your life protesting under the shower-bath that you were actually the husband of the beautiful Countess Prascovie Labinska. Compassionate souls would say on hearing you: Poor Octave! And you would be disowned like Balzac's Chabert who wished to prove he was not dead."

This was all so mathematically true that the discouraged count let his head fall on his breast.

" As you are at present Octave de Saville you have doubtless searched his desk and rummaged among his papers, and you are not ignorant that for three years he has nourished for the Countess Prascovie Labinska a desperate, hopeless love, which he. has tried in vain to tear from his heart, and which will only leave him with his life, unless it follows him to the tomb."

" Yes, I know it," said the count, biting his lip.

" Well, to reach her I have employed terrible means, on which a delirious passion alone would venture. Dr. Cherbonneau has attempted for me a task that would startle the thaumaturgists of the universe. After putting us both to sleep he changed the envelopes of our souls. But in vain! I will return you your body: Prascovie does not love me! Under the husband's form she recognized the lover's soul; her look was the same on the threshold of the conjugal apartment as in the garden of the Villa Salviati."

Octave's tone betrayed such true sorrow that the count had faith in his words.

"I am a lover," added Octave, smiling, "and not a thief, and as the only thing which I desired in this world cannot belong to me, I do not see why I should keep your titles, castles, lands, money, horses, and weapons. There, give me your arm; let us appear reconciled, thank our seconds, take with us Dr. Cherbonneau, and return to the magical laboratory from which we came forth transformed. The old Brahman will know how to undo his work."

"Gentlemen," said Octave, sustaining for a little longer the part of Count Olaf Labinski, "my adversary and I have exchanged confidential explications which render the continuation of the duel useless. There is nothing

like crossing swords a bit to clear the minds
of sensible people."

MM. Zamoieczki and de Sepulveda reën-
tered their carriage, and Alfred Humbert and
Gustave Raimbaud regained theirs, while
Count Olaf Labinski, Octave de Saville, and
Dr. Cherbonneau drove at full speed towards
the Rue du Regard.

.

XII.

DURING the transit from the Bois de Boulogne to the Rue du Regard, Octave de Saville
said to Dr. Cherbonneau, —

" My dear doctor, I am about to test your
science once more ; you must restore our souls,
each to its customary habitation. That should
not be difficult for you. I hope that Count
Labinski will not be angry at you for having
made him change a palace for a hovel, and
lodging his illustrious personality for some
hours in my poor individuality. But then, you
possess a power which fears nothing."

With an acquiescent gesture Dr. Balthazar
Cherbonneau replied : " The operation will be
much simpler this time ; the imperceptible
filaments which hold the soul to the body
have with you been recently broken, and have
not had time to be renewed, and your minds

will not form that obstacle which the instinctive resistance of the magnetized opposes to the magnetizer. The count will doubtless pardon an old erudite like myself for not having been able to resist the pleasure of putting in practice an experiment for which one finds but few subjects, and particularly as this attempt has only served to brilliantly confirm a virtue which carries delicacy to divination and triumphs where every other would have succumbed. If you wish, you can look on this momentary transformation as a strange dream, and perhaps, later, you will not be sorry to have experienced the odd sensation, which few men have known, of having inhabited two bodies. Metempsychosis is not a new doctrine; but before transmigrating into another existence the souls drink the cup of forgetfulness, and every one cannot, like Pythagoras, remember to have assisted at the Trojan war."

"The benefit of being reinstalled in my own individuality," the count answered politely, "equals the unpleasantness of having been expropriated from it; this is said without ill-feeling for M. Octave de Saville, whom I still am, and whom I am about to cease to be."

Octave smiled with the lips of Count Labinski at this sentence which could only reach him through another's envelope, and silence established itself between these three persons whose abnormal situation rendered all conversation difficult.

The unfortunate Octave thought of his vanished hope, and his reflections were not, it must be owned, precisely rose-color. Like all repulsed lovers, he still asked himself why he was not loved — as if love had a why! The only reason one can give it is the *because*, a reply logical in its obstinate laconism, and which women oppose to all embarrassing questions. Nevertheless, he recognized his defeat, and felt that the spring of life, which for an instant Dr. Cherbonneau had renovated for him, was newly broken, and rattled in his heart like that of a watch dropped on the ground. Octave would not have caused his mother the sorrow of his suicide; and he sought a spot wherein he might extinguish his unknown grief quietly under the scientific name of a plausible illness. Had he been an artist, poet, or musician, he would have crystallized his pain in masterpieces; and Prascovie, robed in white, crowned with stars, like Dante's Beatrice, would have hovered about his inspiration like an angel of light; but, as has been intimated at the beginning of this story, though well instructed and gifted, Octave was not one of those chosen spirits who imprint on this earth the trace of their passage. In his obscure sublimity he only knew how to love and die.

The carriage entered the court of the old hotel in the Rue du Regard, a court whose pavement was set in green grass through which the visitors' steps had worn a path, and which the high gray walls of the building inundated with shadow, like that which falls from a clois-ter's arcades; Silence and Immobility, like invisible statues, watched on the threshold protecting the meditations of the erudite.

When Octave and the count had alighted, the physician jumped from the carriage with a lighter step than one would have expected from his age, without even leaning on the arm which the footman offered to him with that politeness which servants of large establishments affect towards old or feeble persons.

As soon as the double doors had closed on them, Olaf and Octave felt themselves wrapped in the hot atmosphere which recalled to the physician that of India, and in which only he could breathe at his ease, but which almost suffocated those who had not, like him, been for thirty years torrified in tropical suns. The incarnations of Vishnu still leered in their frames, weirder by day than by lamplight; Shiva, the blue god, sneered on his pedestal; and Dourga, biting his callous lip with his wild boar's tusks, seemed to agitate his chaplet of skulls. The apartment retained its magical and mysterious appearance. Dr. Balthazar

Cherbonneau led his two subjects to the room where the first transformation had taken place. He turned the glass disk of the electric machine, shook the iron rods of the mesmeric battery, opened the hot-air registers to make the temperature rise rapidly, read two or three lines from parchments so ancient that they resembled old bark ready to crumble into dust, and, when several minutes had elapsed, said to Octave and the count, —

"Gentlemen, I am at your service; shall we begin?"

While the physician was making these preparations, disquieting reflections passed through the count's mind.

"When I am asleep, what is this old lugubrious-faced magician, who might be the devil himself, going to do with my soul? Will he restore it to my body, or will he carry it off to hell with him? Is not this exchange, which ought to give me back my happiness, a Machiavellian combination for some sorcery whose end escapes me? Still, my position could not be worse. Octave possesses my body, and, as he wisely remarked this morning, in reclaiming it with my present figure I should cause myself to be shut up as a lunatic. If he wished to put me definitely out of his way, he had only to drive in the point of his sword; I was disarmed, at his mercy; the justice of man could have said nothing against it; the form of the duel was perfectly regular, and it would have been done all in order. I must think of Prascovie and have no childish fears. Let me try the only way which is left me to regain her!"

And, like Octave, he grasped the rod which Dr. Balthazar Cherbonneau presented to him.

Overpowered by the metal conductors, charged to the utmost with electric fluid, the two young men sank into an unconsciousness so profound that to any one unprepared for it it would have resembled death. The physician made the passes, performed the rites, pronounced the syllables as on the first occasion, and soon two luminous stars appeared above Octave and the count. The physician led to its original abode Count Olaf Labinski's soul, which followed the electrician's gesture with an eager flight.

During this time Octave's soul moved slowly from Olaf's body, and instead of rejoining its own, rose, rose as if glad to be free, and appeared indifferent to its prison. The physician was touched with pity for the fluttering, winged Psyche, and asked himself if it were a kindness to bring it back to this vale of misery. In this momentary hesitation the soul continued to ascend. Remembering his part, M. Cherbonneau repeated with the most imperious accent the irresistible monosyllable, and made a pass pregnant with volition, but the tiny quivering spark was already out of the circle of attraction, and swiftly traversing the upper pane of the window it disappeared.

The physician ceased making efforts which he knew to be useless, and awakened the count, who, seeing himself in a mirror with his usual features, gave a cry of joy, threw a glance at Octave's immobile body to make sure that he was thoroughly clear of that envelope, and with a nod of farewell to M. Balthazar Cherbonneau rushed away.

A few seconds later the muffled roll of a carriage under the arch was heard, and Dr. Balthazar Cherbonneau was alone face to face with the corpse of Octave de Saville.

"By the trunk of Ganesa!" exclaimed the pupil of the Brahman of Elephanta when the count had gone, "this is a provoking affair. I opened the cage-door, the bird flew away, and now it is already beyond the sphere of this world, so far indeed that the Sannyâsi Brahma-Logum himself could not overtake it, and here am I with a corpse on my hands. It is true, I can dissolve it in a corrosive bath of such strength that not an appreciable atom will remain, or I can make of it in a few hours a beautiful mummy, like those inclosed in cases covered with variegated hieroglyphs; but inquiries will be started, my dwelling searched, my chests opened, myself subjected to all sorts of tiresome questions " . . . Here a bright idea crossed the physician's mind ; he seized a pen and wrote rapidly a few lines on a sheet of paper, which he put in the drawer of his table.

The paper contained these words:

" Having neither relatives nor connections, I bequeath all my belongings to M. Octave de Saville, for whom I have a particular affection, on condition that he pays a legacy of one hundred thousand francs to the Brahmanic hospital of Ceylon for old, worn-out, and sick animals ; that he gives twelve hundred francs yearly for life to my Indian and to my English servant; and that he sends the manuscript of the laws of Manu to the Mazarin library."

This testament made to a dead man by a living one is not the strangest thing in this story, improbable yet true; but the singularity of it will be at once explained.

The physician felt Octave de Saville's body, from which the warmth of life had not yet departed, looked in the glass, with a singularly disdainful air, at his own wrinkled face, tanned and rough like a zebra's skin, and making over his head the motion with which one throws off an old coat when the tailor brings a new one, he muttered the formula of the Sannyâsi Brahma-Logum.

Immediately, Dr. Balthazar Cherbonneau's

body fell to the floor as if struck by a thunder-bolt, and that of Octave de Saville rose up in full strength and activity.

Octave-Cherbonneau stood for some minutes before the thin, bony, and livid carcass, which, no longer upheld by the powerful spirit that had before animated it, at once took on a look of complete senility, and rapidly assumed a cadaverous appearance.

" Farewell, poor human remnant, miserable out-at-elbow garment, frayed at every seam, which for seventy years I have dragged about the five parts of the globe !   You did me good service, and I do not leave you without regret. One gets accustomed to living so long together ! but with this young envelope, which my sci-ence will soon make robust, I can study, work, and read still a few words more in the great book before Death, saying 'It is enough!' closes it at the most interesting paragraph ! "

After this funeral oration, addressed to him-self, Octave-Cherbonneau went forth with a tranquil step to take possession of his new existence.

Count Olaf Labinski had returned to his house and had immediately sent to ask if the countess could receive him.

He found her in the conservatory seated on a bank of moss amid a virgin forest of exotic

and tropical plants. The half raised panes
of glass admitted the warm, bright air. She
was reading Novalis, one of the most subtile,
rarefied, and immaterial authors which German spiritualism has produced. The countess
did not like books which paint existence in
strong, real colors ; and, from having lived in a
world of elegance, love, and poetry, life appeared to her a trifle coarse.

She threw down her book and slowly lifted
her eyes to the count. She feared to encounter again in her husband's dark pupils that ardent, stormy look, full of mysterious thoughts,
which had troubled her so much, and which
had seemed to her — foolish apprehension —
the look of another !

In Olaf's eyes shone a serene joy, and a
pure, chaste love burned in them with a steady
fire ; the stranger soul, which had so myste-
riously changed the expression of his features,
was gone forever. Prascovie at once recognized
her adored Olaf, and a quick blush of pleasure
colored her transparent cheeks. Though she
was ignorant of the transformations performed
by Dr. Cherbonneau, her delicate sensitiveness
had unconsciously been aware of all these
changes.

"What are you reading, dear Prascovie ?"
said Olaf, lifting from the moss the book
bound in blue morocco. " Ah I the history

of Henri d'Ofterdingen, — it is the same volume that I went full galop to get you at Mohilev, one day when you had expressed a wish for it at dinner. At midnight it was on the table beside your lamp; but poor Ralph was broken-winded ever after!"

"And I told you that I would never again mention the least desire before you. You have the character of that Spanish noble who prayed his mistress not to gaze at the stars, since he could not give them to her."

"If you looked at one," replied the count, "I should try to climb to heaven and ask it of God."

While listening to her husband the countess smoothed a refractory mesh of her hair which scintillated like a flame in a ray of gold. The motion had disarranged her sleeve, and uncovered her beautiful arm encircled at the wrist by the turquoise-studded lizard which she wore on the day of her apparition in the Cascine so fatal to Octave.

"What a fright that poor little lizard once gave you!" said the count. "It was when you had, on my insistent prayer, descended to the garden for the first time, and I killed it with the stroke of a switch. I had it dipped in gold and decorated with a few stones; but even as a trinket it still appeared disagreeable to you, and it was some time before you could bring yourself to wear it."

"Oh, I am quite accustomed to it now, and it is my favorite ornament, for it recalls a very dear remembrance."

"Yes," replied the count, "on that day we agreed that on the morrow I should make your aunt an official request for your hand."

The countess recognized the look and tone of the real Olaf, and reassured also by these intimate details, she rose smiling, took his arm, and made several turns about the conservatory with him, plucking with free hand as she went some flowers whose petals she pulled off with her fresh lips, looking as she did so like that Venus of Schiavoni's who is feasting on roses.

"As you have such a good memory to-day," she said, flinging from her the flower she had been mutilating with her pearly teeth, "you ought to have recovered the use of your mother-tongue . . . which yesterday you no longer knew."

"If souls retain a human language in paradise," answered the count in Polish, "it is the one my soul will speak in heaven to tell you that I love you."

Prascovie, still moving, let her head fall gently on Olaf's shoulder.

"Dear heart," she murmured, "now you are as I love you to be. Yesterday you frightened me, and I fled as from a stranger."

The next day Octave de Saville, animated by the spirit of the old physician, received a black-edged letter which begged him to assist at the funeral service and burial of M. Balthazar Cherbonneau.

Clothed in his new aspect, the physician followed his former body to the cemetery, saw himself buried, listened with a well-assumed air of regret to the address pronounced over his grave, in which the irreparable loss to science was deplored, and then returned to the Rue Saint Lazare and awaited the opening of the will he had made in his own favor.

That day could be read among the items of the evening papers :

" Dr. Balthazar Cherbonneau, known by his long sojourn in India, his philological knowledge, and his marvelous cures, was yesterday found dead in his laboratory. A most thorough examination of the body has banished all idea of a crime. M. Cherbonneau probably succumbed to excessive mental fatigue, or perished in some audacious experiment. It is said that a will in the testator's own handwriting leaves to the Mazarin library some extremely valuable manuscripts, and names as heir a young man belonging to a distinguished family, M. O. de S."

THE VENUS OF ILLE.

THE VENUS OF ILLE.

Γλεὼς ἦν δέγὼ, ἔστω ὁ ἀνδρίας
καὶ ἤπιος, οὔτως ἀνδρεῖος ὤν.
Λουκιανου Φιλοψευδης.

BY PROSPER MÉRIMÉE.

———◆———

I WAS descending the last slope of the
Canigou, and though the sun was already set
I could distinguish on the plain the houses
of the small town of Ille, towards which I
directed my steps.

"Of course," I said to the Catalan who
since the day before served as my guide, "you
know where M. de Peyrehorade lives?"

"Just don't I," cried he; "I know his
house like my own, and if it were not so dark
I would show it to you. It is the finest in
Ille. He is rich, M. de Peyrehorade is, and
he marries his son to one richer even than
he."

"Does the marriage come off soon?" I
asked him.

"Soon? It may be that the violins are already ordered for the wedding. To-night per-

haps, to-morrow or the next day, how do I
know? It will take place at Puygarrig, for it
is Mademoiselle de Puygarrig that the son is
to marry. It will be a sight, I can tell you."

I was recommended to M. de Peyrehorade
by my friend M. de P. He was, I had been
told, an antiquarian of much learning and a
man of charming affability. He would take
delight in showing me the ruins for ten leagues
around. Therefore I counted on him to visit
the outskirts of Ille, which I knew to be rich
in memorials of the Middle Ages. This marriage, of which I now heard for the first time,
upset all my plans.

"I shall be a troublesome guest, I told
myself. But I am expected; my arrival has
been announced by M. de P.: I must present
myself."

When we reached the plain the guide said,
"Wager a cigar, sir, that I can guess what you
are going to do at M. de Peyrehorade's."

Offering him one, I answered, "It is not very
hard to guess. At this hour, when one has
made six leagues in the Canigou, supper is the
great thing after all."

"Yes, but to-morrow? Here I wager that
you have come to Ille to see the idol. I
guessed that when I saw you draw the portraits of the saints at Serrabona."

"The idol! what idol?" This word had
aroused my curiosity.

"What! were you not told at Perpignan how M. de Peyrehorade had found an idol in the earth?"

"You mean to say an earthen statue?"

"Not at all. A statue in copper, and there is enough of it to make a lot of big pennies. She weighs as much as a church-bell. It was deep in the ground at the foot of an olive-tree that we got her."

"You were present at the discovery?"

"Yes, sir. Two weeks ago M. de Peyrehorade told Jean Coll and me to uproot an old olive-tree which was frozen last year when the weather as you know was very severe. So in working, Jean Coll, who went at it with all his might, gave a blow with his pickaxe, and I heard *binn* — as if he had struck a bell, and I said, What is that? We dug on and on, and there was a black hand, which looked like the hand of a corpse, sticking out of the earth. I was scared to death. I ran to M. de Peyrehorade and I said to him, — 'There are dead people, master, under the olive-tree! The priest must be called.'

"'What dead people,' said he to me. He came, and he had no sooner seen the hand, than he cried out 'An antique! an antique!' You would have thought he had found a treasure. And there he was with the pickaxe in his own hands, struggling and doing almost as much work as we two."

"And at last what did you find?"

"A huge black woman more than half naked, with due respect to you, sir. She was all in copper, and M. de Peyrehorade told us it was an idol of pagan times — the time of Charlemagne."

"I see what it is, — some virgin or other in bronze from a destroyed convent."

"A virgin! Had it been one I should have recognized it. It is an idol, I tell you; you can see it in her look. She fixes you with her great white eyes — one might say she stares at you. One lowers one's eyes, yes indeed one does, on looking at her."

"White eyes? Doubtless they are set in the bronze. Perhaps it is some Roman statue."

"Roman! That's it. M. de Peyrehorade says it is Roman. Oh! I see you are an erudite like himself."

"Is she complete, well preserved?"

"Yes, sir, she lacks nothing. It is a handsomer statue and better finished than the bust of Louis Philippe in colored plaster which is in the town-hall. But with all that the face of the idol does not please me. She has a wicked expression, — and, what is more, she is wicked."

"Wicked! what has she done to you?"

"Nothing to me exactly; but wait a minute. We had gotten down on all fours to stand her

upright, and M. de Peyrehorade was also pull-
ing on the rope, though he has not much more
strength than a chicken. With much trouble
we got her up straight. I reached for a
broken tile to support her, when if she does n't
tumble over backwards all in a heap. I said,
'take care,' but not quick enough, for Jean
did not have time to draw away his leg " —

" And it was hurt ? "

" Broken as clean as a vine-prop. When I
saw that I was furious, I wanted to take my
pickaxe and smash the statue to pieces, but
M. de Peyrehorade stopped me. He gave
Jean Coll some money, but all the same, he is
in bed still, though it is two weeks since it
happened, and the physician says that he will
never walk as well with that leg as with the
other. It is a pity, for he was our best runner,
and, after M. de Peyrehorade's son, the clever-
est racquet player. M. Alphonse de Peyrehorade was sorry I can tell you, for Coll always
played on his side. It was beautiful to see
how they returned each other the balls. They
never touched the ground."

Chatting in this way we entered Ille, and I
soon found myself in the presence of M. de
Peyrehorade. He was a little old man, still
hale and active, with powdered hair, a red
nose, and a jovial, bantering manner. Before opening M. de P.'s letter he had seated

me at a well-spread table, and had presented
me to his wife and son as a célebrated archæologist who was to draw Roussillon from the
neglect in which the indifference of erudites
had left it.

While eating heartily, for nothing makes
one hungrier than the keen air of the mountains, I scrutinized my hosts.   I have said a
word about M. de Peyrehorade, I must add
that he was activity personified.   He talked,
got up, ran to his library, brought me books,
showed me engravings, and filled my glass, all
at the same time.   He was never two minutes in repose.   His wife was a trifle stout, as
are most Catalans when they are over forty
years of age.   She appeared to me a thorough
provincial, solely occupied with her house-
keeping.   Though the supper was sufficient
for at least six persons, she hurried to the
kitchen and had pigeons killed and a number
broiled, and she opened I do not know how
many jars of preserves.   In no time the table
was laden with dishes and bottles, and if I
had but tasted of everything offered me I
should certainly have died of indigestion.
Nevertheless, at each dish I refused they made
fresh excuses.   They feared I found myself
very badly off at Ille.   In the provinces there
were so few resources, and of course Parisians
were fastidious !

In the midst of his parent's comings and goings M. Alphonse de Peyrehorade was as immovable as rent-day. He was a tall young man of twenty-six, with a regular and handsome countenance, but lacking in expression. His height and his athletic figure well justified the reputation of an indefatigable racquet player given him in the neighborhood.

On that evening he was dressed in an elegant manner ; that is to say, he was an exact copy of a fashion plate in the last number of the *Journal des Modes.* But he seemed to me ill at ease in his clothes ; he was as stiff as a post in his velvet collar, and could only turn all of a piece. In striking contrast to his costume were his large sunburnt hands and blunt nails. They were a laborer's hands issuing from the sleeves of an exquisite. Moreover, though he examined me in my quality of Parisian most curiously from head to foot, he only spoke to me once during the whole evening, and that was to ask me where I had bought my watch-chain.

As the supper was drawing to an end M. de Peyrehorade said to me : " Ah ! my dear guest, you belong to me now you are here. I shall not let go of you until you have seen everything of interest in our mountains. You must learn to know our Roussillon, and to do it justice. You do not suspect all that we have to show you, Phœnician, Celtic, Roman, Arabian, and Byzantine monuments ; you shall see them all from the cedar to the hyssop. I shall drag you everywhere, and will not spare you a single stone."

A fit of coughing obliged him to pause. I took advantage of it to tell him that I should be sorry to disturb him on an occasion of so much interest to his family. If he would but give me his excellent advice about the excursions to be made, I could, without his taking the trouble to accompany me.

"Ah! you mean the marriage of that boy there," he exclaimed, interrupting me ; "stuff and nonsense, it will be over the day after to-morrow. You will go to the wedding with us, which is to be informal, as the bride is in mourning for an aunt whose heiress she is. Therefore, there will be no festivities, no ball. It is a pity, though ; you might have seen our Catalans dance. They are pretty, and might have given you the desire to imitate Alphonse. One marriage they say leads to another. Once the young people married I shall be free, and we will bestir ourselves. I beg your pardon for boring you with a provincial wedding. For a Parisian tired of entertainments — and a wedding without a ball at that! Still you will see a bride — a bride — well, you shall tell me what you think of her. But you are a thinker and no longer notice women. I have better than that to show you. You shall see something; in fact, I have a fine surprise in store for you to-morrow."

"Good heavens!" said I; "it is difficult to have a treasure in the house without the public being aware of it. I think I know the surprise in reserve for me. But if it is your statue which is in question, the description my guide gave me of it has only served to excite my curiosity and prepared me to admire."

"Ah! So he spoke to you about the idol, as he calls my beautiful Venus Tur; but I will tell you nothing. To-morrow you shall see her by daylight, and tell me if I am right in thinking the statue a masterpiece. You could not have arrived more opportunely. There are inscriptions on it which I, poor ignoramus that I am, explain after my own fashion; but you, a Parisian erudite, will probably laugh at my interpretation; for I have actually written a paper about it, — I, an old provincial antiquary, have launched myself in literature. I wish to make the press groan. If you would kindly read and correct it I might have some hope. For example, I am very anxious to know how you translate this inscription from the base of the statue: CAVE. But I do not wish to ask you yet! Wait until to-morrow. Not a word more about the Venus to-day!"

" You are right, Peyrehorade," said his wife ;
" drop your idol. Can you not see that you
prevent our guest from eating? You may be
sure that he has seen in Paris much finer
statues than yours. In the Tuilleries there are
dozens, and they also are in bronze."

" There you have the saintly ignorance of
the provinces !" interrupted M. de Peyrehorade.
" The idea of comparing an admirable antique
to the insipid figures of Coustou !

> ' How irreverently my housekeeper
> Speaks of the gods ! '

Do you know that my wife wanted me to melt
my statue into a bell for our church. She would
have been the godmother. Just think of it, to
melt a masterpiece by Myron, sir ! "

" Masterpiece ! Masterpiece ! A charming
masterpiece she is ! to break a man's leg."

" Madam, do you see that ? " said M. de
Peyrehorade in a resolute tone, extending toward her his right leg in its changeable silk
stocking ; " if my Venus had broken that leg
there for me I should not regret it."

" Good gracious ! Peyrehorade, how can
you say such a thing ! Fortunately, the man is
better. And yet I cannot bring myself to look
at a statue which has caused so great a disas-
ter. Poor Jean Coll ! "

" Wounded by Venus, sir," said M. de Peyre-

horade, with a loud laugh ; " wounded by Venus,
and the churl complains !

'Veneris nec præmia nôris.'

Who has not been wounded by Venus ? "

M. Alphonse, who understood French better
than Latin, winked one eye with an air of intelligence, and looked at me as if to ask, " And
you, Parisian, do you understand ? "

The supper came to an end. I had ceased
eating an hour before. I was weary, and I
could not manage to hide the frequent yawns
which escaped me. Madame de Peyrehorade
was the first to notice them, and remarked that
it was time to go to bed. Then followed fresh
apologies for the poor accommodations I would
have. I would not be as well off as in Paris.
It was so uncomfortable in the provinces!
Indulgence was needed for the Roussillonnais.
Notwithstanding my protests that after a tramp
in the mountains a bundle of straw would
seem to me a delicious couch, they continued
begging me to pardon poor country people if
they did not treat me as well as they could
have wished.

Accompanied by M. de Peyrehorade I ascended at last to the room arranged for me.
The staircase, the upper half of which was in
wood, ended in the centre of a hall, out of
which opened several rooms.

"To the right," said my host, "is the apartment which I propose to give the future Madame Alphonse. Your room is at the opposite end of the corridor. You understand," he added in a manner which he meant to be sly, — "you understand that newly married people must be alone. You are at one end of the house, they at the other."

We entered a well-furnished room where the first object on which my gaze rested was a bed seven feet long, six wide, and so high that one needed a chair to climb up into it.

Having shown me where the bell was, and assured himself that the sugar-bowl was full and the cologne bottles duly placed on the toilet-stand, my host asked me a number of times if anything was lacking, wished me good night, and left me alone.

The windows were closed. Before undressing I opened one to breathe the fresh night air so delightful after a long supper. Facing me was the Canigou. Always magnificent, it appeared to me on that particular evening, lighted as it was by a resplendent moon, as the most beautiful mountain in the world. I remained a few minutes contemplating its marvelous silhouette, and was about to close the window when, lowering my eyes, I perceived a dozen yards from the house the statue on its pedestal. It was placed at the

corner of a hedge that separated a small garden from a vast, perfectly level quadrangle,
which I learned later was the racquet court
of the town. This ground was the property
of M. de Peyrehorade, and had been given by
him to the parish at the solicitation of his son.

Owing to the distance it was difficult for me
to distinguish the attitude of the statue; I
could only judge of its height, which seemed
to be about six feet. At that moment two
scamps of the town, whistling the pretty Roussillon tune, *Montagnes régalades,* were crossing
the racquet court quite near the hedge. They
paused to look at the statue, and one of them
even apostrophized it aloud. He spoke Cata-
lonian, but I had been long enough in Roussillon to understand pretty well what he said.

"There you are, you wench!" (The Cata-
lonian word was much more forcible.) "There
you are!" he said. "It was you then who
broke Jean Coll's leg! If you belonged to me
I'd break your neck."

"Bah! what with?" said the other youth.
"It is of the copper of pagan times, and harder
than I don't know what."

"If I had my chisel" (it seems he was a
locksmith's apprentice), "I would soon force
out its big white eyes, as I would pop an al-
mond from its shell. There are more than a
hundred pennies' worth of silver in them."

They went on a few steps.

"I must wish the idol good - night," said the taller of the apprentices, stopping suddenly.

He stooped and probably picked up a stone. I saw him unbend his arm and throw something. A blow resounded on the bronze, and immediately the apprentice raised his hand to his head with a cry of pain.

"She threw it back at me!" he exclaimed. And my two rascals ran off as fast as they could. It was evident that the stone had rebounded from the metal and had punished the wag for the outrage he had done the goddess. Laughing heartily, I shut the window.

Another Vandal punished by Venus! May all the desecrators of our old monuments thus get their due!

With this charitable wish I fell asleep.

When I awoke it was broad day. On one side of my bed stood M. de Peyrehorade in a dressing-gown; a servant sent by his wife was on the other side with a cup of chocolate in his hand.

"Come, come, you Parisian, get up! This is quite the laziness of the capital!" said my host, while I dressed in haste. "It is eight o'clock, and you are still in bed! I have been up since six. This is the third time I have been to your door. I approached on tiptoe:

no one, not a sign of life. It is bad for you to
sleep too much at your age. And my Venus,
which you have not yet seen ! Come, hurry up
and take this cup of Barcelona chocolate. It
is real contraband chocolate, such as cannot
be found in Paris. Prepare yourself, for when
you are once before my Venus no one will be
able to tear you away from her."

I was ready in five minutes, that is to say,
I was half shaved, half dressed, and burnt by
the boiling chocolate I had swallowed. I descended to the garden and saw an admirable
statue before me. It was truly a Venus, and
of marvelous beauty. The upper part of the
body was nude, as great divinities were usually
represented by the ancients. The right hand
was raised as high as the breast, the palm
turned inwards, the thumb and two first fingers extended, and the others slightly bent.
The other hand, drawn close to the hip, held
the drapery which covered the lower half of
the body. The attitude of this statue reminded
one of that of the *mourre* player which is
called, I hardly know why, by the name of
Germanicus. Perhaps it had been intended
to represent the goddess as playing at *mourre*.
However that may be, it is impossible to find
anything more perfect than the form of this
Venus, anything softer and more voluptuous
than her outlines, or more graceful and dig-

nified than her drapery. I had expected·a work of the decadence; I saw a masterpiece of statuary's best days.

What struck me most was the exquisite reality of the figure; one might have thought it moulded from life, that is, if Nature ever produced such perfect models.

The hair, drawn back from the brow, seemed once to have been gilded. The head was small, like nearly all those of Greek statues, and bent slightly forward. As to the face, I shall never succeed in describing its strange character; it was of a type belonging to no other Greek statue which I can remember. It had not the calm, severe beauty of the Greek sculptors, who systematically gave a majestic immobility to all the features. On the contrary, I noticed here, with surprise, a marked intention on the artist's part to reproduce malice verging on viciousness. All the features were slightly contracted. The eyes were rather oblique, the mouth raised at the corners, the nostrils a trifle dilated. Disdain, irony, and cruelty were to be read in the nevertheless beautiful face.

Truly, the more one gazed at the statue the more one experienced a feeling of pain that such wonderful beauty could be allied to such an absence of all sensibility.

"If the model ever existed," I said to M. de

Peyrehorade, "and I doubt if heaven ever produced such a woman, how I pity her lovers! She must have taken pleasure in making them die of despair. There is something ferocious in her expression, and yet I have never seen anything more beautiful."

"'*C'est Venus tout entière à sa proie attachée!*'" cried M. de Peyrehorade, delighted with my enthusiasm.

But the expression of demoniac irony was perhaps increased by the contrast of the bright silver eyes with the dusky green hue which time had given to the statue. The shining eyes produced a sort of illusion which simulated reality and life. I remembered what my guide had said, that those who looked at her were forced to lower their eyes. It was almost true, and I could not prevent a movement of anger at myself when I felt ill at ease before this bronze figure.

"Now that you have seen everything in detail, my dear colleague in antiquities, let us, if you please, open a scientific conference. What do you say to this inscription which you have not yet noticed?" He pointed to the base of the statue, and I read these words:

CAVE AMANTEM.

"*Quid dicis doctissime?*" he asked, rubbing his hands. "Let us see if we agree as to the meaning of *cave amantem!*"

"But," I replied, "it has two meanings. You can translate it : 'Guard against him who loves thee,' that is, 'distrust lovers.' But in this sense I do not know if *cave amantem* would be good Latin. After seeing the diabolical expression of the lady I should sooner believe that the artist meant to warn the spectator against this terrible beauty. I should then translate it : 'Take care of thyself if *she* loves thee.'"

"Humph !" said M. de Peyrehorade; "yes, it is an admissible meaning : but, if you do not mind, I prefer the first translation, which I would, however, develop. You know Venus's lover ? "

"There are several."

"Yes; but the first is Vulcan. Why should it not mean : 'Notwithstanding all thy beauty, thine air of disdain, thou wilt have a blacksmith, a wretched cripple for a lover'? A profound lesson, sir, for coquettes !"

The explication seemed so far-fetched that I could not help smiling.

To avoid formally contradicting my antiquarian friend, I observed, "Latin is a terrible language in its conciseness," and I drew back several steps to better contemplate the statue.

"Wait a moment, colleague !" said M. de Peyrehorade, catching hold of my arm; "you have not seen all. There is another inscription. Climb up on the pedestal and look at the right arm." So saying, he helped me up, and without much ceremony I clung to the neck of the Venus with whom I was becoming more familiar. For a second I even looked her straight in the eyes, and on close inspection she appeared more wicked, and, if possible, more beautiful than before. Then I noticed that on the arm were engraved, as it seemed to me, characters in ancient script. With the aid of my spectacles I spelt out what follows, and M. de Peyrehorade, approving with voice and gesture, repeated each word as I uttered it. Thus I read :

> VENERI TVRBVL . . .
> EVTVCHES MYRO.
> IMPERIO FECIT.

After the word 'Tvrbvl' in the first line it looked to me as if there were several letters effaced ; but 'Tvrbvl' was perfectly legible.

"Which means to say?" my host asked radiantly, with a mischievous smile, for he thought the 'Tvrbvl' would puzzle me.

"There is one word which I do not yet understand," I answered ; "all the rest is simple. Eutyches Myron has made this offering to Venus by her command."

"Quite right. But 'Tvrbvl,' what do you make of it? What does it mean ?"

"'Tvrbvl' perplexes me very much. I am

trying to think of one of Venus's familiar char-
acteristics which may enlighten me. But what
do you say to 'Tvrbvlenta'? The Venus who
troubles, agitates. You see I am still preoccupied by her wicked expression. 'Tvrbvlenta'
is not too bad a quality for Venus," I added
modestly, for I was not too well satisfied with
my explanation.

"A turbulent Venus! A noisy Venus! Ah!
then you think my Venus is a public-house
Venus? Nothing of the kind, sir; she is a
Venus of good society. I will explain 'Tvrbvl' to you — that is, if you promise me not
to divulge my discovery before my article ap-
pears in print. Because, you see, I pride myself on such a find, and, after all, you Parisian
erudites are rich enough to leave a few ears
for us poor devils of provincials to glean!"

From the top of the pedestal, where I was
still perched, I promised him solemnly that I
would never be so base as to filch from him
his discovery.

"'Tvrbvl,'— sir," said he, coming nearer and
lowering his voice for fear some one besides
myself might hear him, "read 'Tvrbvlneræ.'"

"I understand no better."

"Listen to me attentively. Three miles
from here at the foot of the mountain is a
village called Boulternère. The name is a
corruption of the Latin word 'Tvrbvlnera.'

Nothing is more common than these transpositions. Boulternère was a Roman town. I always suspected it, but I could get no proof till now, and here it is. This Venus was the local goddess of the city of Boulternère; and the word Boulternère, which I have shown is of ancient origin, proves something very curious, namely, that Boulternère was a Phœnician town before it was Roman!"

He paused a moment to take breath and enjoy my surprise. I succeeded in overcoming a strong inclination to laugh.

"'Tvrbvlnera' is, in fact, pure Phœnician," he continued. "'Tvr,' pronounce 'tour'— 'Tour' and 'Sour' are the same word, are they not? 'Sour' is the Phœnician name of Tyr; I do not need to recall the meaning to you. 'Bvl' is Baal; Bâl, Bel, Bul are slight differences of pronunciation. As to 'Nera,' that troubles me a little. I am tempted to believe, for want of a Phœnician word, that it comes from the Greek νηρός, moist, marshy. In that case, it is a mongrel word. To justify νηρός I will show you at Boulternère how the mountain streams form stagnant pools. Then, again, the ending 'Nera' may have been added much later in honor of Nera Pivesuvia, wife of Tetricus, who may have benefited the city of Turbul. But on account of the marshes, I prefer the etymology of νηρός."

He took a pinch of snuff in a complacent way, and continued :

"But let us leave the Phœnicians and return to the inscription. I translate it then : To Venus of Boulternère Myron dedicates by her order this statue, his work."

I took good care not to criticise his etymology, but I wished in my turn to give a proof of penetration, so I said, —

"Stop a moment, M.de Peyrehorade. Myron has dedicated something, but I by no means see that it is this statue."

"What ! " he cried, " was not Myron a famous Greek sculptor ? The talent was perpetuated in his family, and it must have been one of his descendants who executed this statue. Nothing can be more certain."

"But," I replied, "on this arm I see a small hole. I think it served to fasten something, a bracelet for example, which this Myron, being an unhappy lover, gave to Venus as an expiatory offering. Venus was irritated against him ; he appeased her by consecrating to her a gold bracelet. Notice that *fecit* is often used for *consecravit*. The terms are synonymous. I could show you more than one example if I had at hand Gruter or Orellius. It is natural that a lover should see Venus in a dream and imagine that she commands him to give a gold bracelet to her statue. Myron consecrated the bracelet to her. Then the barbarians or some other sacrilegious thieves " —

" Ah ! it is easy to see you have written romances ! " cried my host, helping me down from the pedestal. " No, sir ; it is a work of Myron's school. You have only to look at the workmanship to be convinced of that."

Having made it a rule never to contradict self-opinionated antiquarians, I bowed with an air of conviction, saying, —

" It is an admirable piece of work."

"Good heavens ! " exclaimed M. de Peyre-horade, "another act of vandalism ! Some one must have thrown a stone at my statue ! "

He had just perceived a white mark a little above the bosom of the Venus. I noticed a similar mark on the fingers of the right hand. I supposed it had been touched by the stone as it passed, or that a bit of the stone had been broken off as it struck the statue, and had rebounded on the hand. I told my host of the insult I had witnessed, and the prompt punishment which had followed it.

He laughed heartily, and, comparing the apprentice to Diomede, wished he might, like the Greek hero, see all his comrades turned into white birds.

The breakfast bell interrupted this classical conversation, and, as on the preceding evening, I was obliged to eat enough for four. Then came M. de Peyrehorade's farmers, and, while he was giving them an audience, his son led me to inspect an open carriage, which he had bought at Toulouse for his betrothed, and which it is needless to say I duly admired. After that I went into the stable with him, where he kept me a half hour, boasting about his horses, giving me their genealogy, and telling me of the prizes they had won at the county races. At last he began to talk to me about his betrothed in connection with a gray mare which he intended for her.

"We will see her to-day," he said. "I do not know if you will find her pretty. In Paris people are hard to please. But every one here and in Perpignan thinks her lovely. The best of it is that she is very rich. Her aunt from Prades left her a fortune. Oh! I shall be very happy."

I was profoundly shocked to see a young man appear more affected by the dower than by the beauty of his bride.

"You are a judge of jewels," continued M. Alphonse; "what do you think of this? Here is the ring I shall give her to-morrow."

He drew from his little finger a heavy ring, enriched with diamonds, and fashioned into two clasped hands, an allusion which seemed to me infinitely poetic. The workmanship was antique, but I fancied it had been retouched to insert the diamonds. Inside the ring these words in Gothic characters could be discerned : *Sempr' ab ti*, which means, thine forever.

"It is a pretty ring," I said, "but the diamonds which have been added have made it lose a little of its style."

"Oh! it is much handsomer now," he answered, smiling. "There are twelve hundred francs' worth of diamonds in it. My mother gave it to me. It is a very old family ring, — it dates from the days of chivalry. It was my grandmother's, who had it from her grandmother. Heaven knows when it was made."

"The custom in Paris," I said, "is to give a perfectly plain ring, usually composed of two different metals, such as gold and platina. The other ring which you have on would be very suitable. This one with its diamonds and its clasped hands is so thick that it would be impossible to wear a glove over it."

"Madame Alphonse must arrange that as she pleases. I think she will be very glad to have it all the same. Twelve hundred francs on the finger is pleasant. That other little ring," he added, looking in a contented way at the plain ring he wore, "that one a woman in Paris gave me on Shrove Tuesday. How I did enjoy myself when I was in Paris two years ago! That is the place to have a good time!" and he sighed regretfully.

We were to dine that day at Puygarrig, with the relations of the bride; so we got in the carriage, and drove to the château, which was four or five miles from Ille. I was presented and received as the friend of the family. I will not speak of the dinner, or the conversation which followed. I took but little part in it. M. Alphonse was seated beside his betrothed, and whispered a word or two in her ear now and then. As for her, she hardly raised her eyes; and every time her lover spoke to her she blushed modestly, but answered without embarrassment.

Mademoiselle de Puygarrig was eighteen years of age. Her slender, graceful figure formed a striking contrast to the stalwart frame of her future husband. She was not only beautiful, she was alluring. I admired the perfect naturalness of all her replies. Her kind look, which yet was not free from a touch of malice, reminded me, in spite of myself, of my host's Venus. While making this inward comparison, I asked myself if the incontestably superior beauty of the statue did not in great measure come from its tigress-like expression; for strength, even in evil passions, always arouses in us astonishment, and a sort of involuntary admiration.

"What a pity," I thought, on leaving Puygarrig, "that such an attractive girl should be

rich, and that her dowry makes her sought by
a man quite unworthy of her."

While returning to Ille, I spoke to Mme.
de Peyrehorade, to whom I thought it only
proper to address myself now and then, though
I did not very well know what to say to her:
" You must be strong-minded people in Roussillon," I said. " How is it, madam, that you
have a wedding on a Friday? We would be
more superstitious in Paris; no one would
dare be married on that day."

" Do not speak of it," she replied ; " if it had
depended on me, certainly another day would
have been chosen. But Peyrehorade wished
it, and I had to give in. All the same, it
troubles me very much. Supposing an accident should happen? There must be some
reason in it, or else why is every one afraid of
Friday? "

" Friday! " cried her husband, " is Venus'
day! Just the day for a wedding! You see,
my dear colleague, I think only of my Venus.
I chose Friday on her account. To-morrow,
if you like, before the wedding, we will make a
little sacrifice to her — a sacrifice of two doves
— and if I only knew where to get some incense " —

" For shame, Peyrehorade! " interrupted his
wife, scandalized to the last degree. " Incense
to an idol! It would be an abomination !

What would they say of us in the neighborhood?"

"At least," answered M. de Peyrehorade, "you will allow me to place a wreath of roses and lilies on her head: *Manibus date lilia plenis.* You see, sir, freedom is an empty word. We have not liberty of worship!"

The next day's arrangements were ordered in the following manner: Every one was to be dressed and ready at ten o'clock punctually. After the chocolate had been served we were to be driven to Puygarrig. The civil marriage was to take place in the town-hall of the village, and the religious ceremony in the chapel of the château. Afterwards there would be a breakfast. After the breakfast people would pass the time as they liked until seven o'clock. At that hour every one would return to M. de Peyrehorade's at Ille, where the two families were to assemble and have supper. It was natural that being unable to dance they should wish to eat as much as possible.

By eight o'clock I was seated in front of the Venus, pencil in hand, recommencing the head of the statue for the twentieth time without being able to catch the expression. M. de Peyrehorade came and went about me, giving me advice, repeating his Phœnician etymology, and laying Bengal roses on the pedestal of the

statue while he addressed vows to it in a tragi-
comic tone for the young couple who were
to live under his roof. Towards nine o'clock
he went in to put on his best, and at the
same moment M. Alphonse appeared looking
very stiff in a new coat, white gloves, chased
sleeve-buttons, and varnished shoes. A rose
decorated his buttonhole.

"Will you make my wife's portrait?" he
asked, leaning over my drawing. "She also is
pretty."

On the racquet-court of which I have spoken
there now began a game which immediately
attracted M. Alphonse's attention. And I,
tired, and despairing of ever being able to copy
the diabolical face, soon left my drawing to
look at the players. There were among them
some Spanish muleteers who had arrived the
night before. They were from Aragon and
Navarre, and were nearly all marvelously skillful at the game. Therefore the Illois, though
encouraged by the presence and advice of M.
Alphonse, were promptly beaten by the foreign champions. The native spectators were
disheartened. M. Alphonse looked at his
watch. It was only half-past nine. His
mother's hair he knew was not dressed. He
hesitated no longer, but taking off his coat
asked for a jacket, and defied the Spaniards.
I looked on smiling and a little surprised.

"The honor of the country must be sustained," he said.

Then I thought him really handsome. He seemed full of life, and his costume, which but now occupied him so entirely, no longer concerned him. A few minutes before he would have dreaded to turn his head for fear of disarranging his cravat. Now he did not give a thought to his curled hair or his fine shirt-front. And his betrothed? If it had been necessary I think he would have postponed the wedding. I saw him hurriedly put on a pair of sandals, roll up his sleeves, and, with an assured air, take his stand at the head of the vanquished party like Cæsar rallying his soldiers at Dyrrachium. I leaped the hedge and placed myself comfortably in the shade of a tree so as to command a good view of both sides.

Contrary to general expectation, M. Alphonse missed the first ball. It came skimming along the ground, it is true, and was thrown with astonishing force by an Aragonese who appeared to be the leader of the Spaniards.

He was a man of about forty, nervous and agile, and at least six feet tall. His olive skin was almost as dark as the bronze of the Venus.

M. Alphonse threw his racquet angrily on the ground.

"It is this cursed ring," he cried, "which

squeezes my finger, and makes me miss a sure ball."

He drew off his diamond ring with some difficulty; I approached to take it, but he forestalled me by running to the Venus and shoving it on her fourth finger. He then resumed his post at the head of the Illois.

He was pale, but calm and resolute. From that moment he did not miss a single ball, and the Spaniards were completely beaten. The enthusiasm of the spectators was a fine sight: some threw their caps in the air and shouted for joy, while others wrung M. Alphonse's hands, calling him the honor of the country. If he had repulsed an invasion I doubt if he would have received warmer or sincerer congratulations. The vexation of the vanquished added to the splendor of the victory.

" We will play other games, my good fellow," he said to the Aragonese in a tone of superiority, "but I will give you points."

I should have wished M. Alphonse to be more modest, and I was almost pained by his rival's humiliation.

The Spanish giant felt the insult deeply. I saw him pale beneath his tan. He looked sullenly at his racquet and clinched his teeth, then, in a smothered voice he muttered:

" *Me lo pagarás.*"

M. de Peyrehorade's voice interrupted his

son's triumph.   Astonished at not finding him
presiding over the preparation of the new
carriage, my host was even more surprised on
seeing him racquet in hand and bathed in perspiration.   M. Alphonse hurried to the house,
washed his hands and face, put on again his
new coat and patent-leather shoes, and in five
minutes we were galloping on the road to
Puygarrig.   All the racquet players of the town
and a crowd of spectators followed us with
shouts of joy.   The strong horses which drew
us could hardly keep ahead of the intrepid
Catalans.

We were at Puygarrig, and the procession
was about to set out for the town-hall, when
M. Alphonse, striking his forehead, whispered
to me :

"What a mess !   I have forgotten the ring !
It is on the finger of the Venus ; may the devil
carry her off !   Do not tell my mother at any
rate.   Perhaps she will not notice it."

"You can send some one for it," I replied.

"My servant remained at Ille.   I do not
trust these here.   Twelve hundred francs' worth
of diamonds might well tempt almost any one.
Moreover, what would they think of my forgetfulness.   They would laugh at me.   They
would call me the husband of the statue.   If it
only is not stolen !   Fortunately, the rascals are
afraid of the idol.   They do not dare approach

it by an arm's length. After all, it does not matter; I have another ring."

The two ceremonies, civil and religious, were accomplished with suitable pomp, and Mademoiselle de Puygarrig received the ring of a Parisian milliner without suspecting that her betrothed was making her the sacrifice of a love-token. Then we seated ourselves at table, where we ate, drank, and even sang, all at great length. I suffered for the bride at the coarse merriment which exploded around her; still, she faced it better than I would have expected, and her embarrassment was neither awkward nor affected.

Perhaps courage comes with difficult situations.

The breakfast ended when heaven pleased. It was four o'clock. The men went to walk in the park, which was magnificent, or watched the peasants, in their holiday attire, dance on the lawn of the château. In this way we passed several hours. Meanwhile, the women were eagerly attentive to the bride, who showed them her presents. Then she changed her dress, and I noticed that she had covered her beautiful hair with a be-feathered bonnet; for women are in no greater hurry than to assume, as soon as possible, the attire which custom forbids their wearing while they are still young girls.

It was nearly eight o'clock when preparations were made to start for Ille. But first a pathetic scene took place. Mlle. de Puygarrig's aunt, a very old and pious woman, who stood to her in a mother's place, was not to go with us. Before the departure she gave her niece a touching sermon on her wifely duties, from which sermon resulted a flood of tears and endless embraces.

M. de Peyrehorade compared this separation to the Rape of the Sabines.

At last, however, we got off, and, on the way, every one exerted himself to amuse the bride and make her laugh ; but all in vain.

At Ille supper awaited us, and what a supper ! If the coarse jokes of the morning had shocked me, I was now much more so by the equivocations and pleasantries of which the bride and groom were the principal objects. The bridegroom, who had disappeared for a moment before seating himself at the table, was pale, cold, and grave.

He drank incessantly some old Collioure wine almost as strong as brandy. I sat next to him, and thought myself obliged to warn him. " Be careful! they say that wine " — I hardly know what stupid nonsense I said to be in harmony with the other guests.

He touched my knee, and whispered :

"When we have left the table . . . let me have two words with you."

His solemn tone surprised me. I looked more closely at him, and noticed a strange alteration in his features.

" Do you feel ill ? " I asked.

" No."

And he began to drink again.

Meanwhile, amidst much shouting and clapping of hands, a child of twelve, who had slipped under the table, held up to the company a pretty pink and white ribbon which he had untied from the bride's ankle. It was called her garter, and at once cut into pieces and distributed among the young men, who, following an old custom still preserved in some patriarchal families, ornamented their buttonholes with it. This was the time for the bride to flush up to the whites of her eyes. But her confusion was at its height when M. de Peyrehorade, having called for silence, sang several verses in Catalan, which he said were impromptu. Here is the meaning, if I understood it correctly :

"What is this, my friends ? has the wine I have drunk made me see double ? There are two Venuses here " . . .

The bridegroom turned his head suddenly with a frightened look, which made every one laugh.

"Yes," continued M. de Peyrehorade, "there are two Venuses under my roof. The one, I found in the ground like a truffle; the other, descended from heaven, has just divided among us her belt."

He meant her garter.

"My son, choose between the Roman Venus and the Catalan the one you prefer. The rascal takes the Catalan, and his choice is the best. The Roman is black, the Catalan is white. The Roman is cold, the Catalan enflames all who approach her."

This equivocal allusion excited such a shout, such noisy applause, and sonorous laughter, that I thought the ceiling would fall on our heads. Around the table there were but three serious faces, those of the newly married couple and mine. I had a terrible headache; and besides, I do not know why, a wedding always saddens me. This one, moreover, even disgusted me a little.

The final verses having been sung, and very lively they were, I must say, every one adjourned to the drawing-room to enjoy the withdrawal of the bride, who, as it was nearly midnight, was soon to be conducted to her room.

M. Alphonse drew me into the embrasure of a window, and, turning away his eyes, said, —

"You will laugh at me — But I don't know what is the matter with me . . . I am bewitched!"

My first thought was that he fancied himself threatened with one of those misfortunes of which Montaigne and Madame de Sévigné speak :

" All the world of love is full of tragic histories," etc.

" I thought only clever people were subject to this sort of accident," I said to myself.

To him I said : " You drank too much Collioure wine, my dear Monsieur Alphonse ; I warned you against it."

" Yes, perhaps. But something much more terrible than that has happened."

His voice was broken. I thought him completely inebriated.

" You know about my ring ? " he continued, after a pause.

" Well, has it been stolen ? "

" No."

" Then you have it ? "

" No — I — I cannot get it off the finger of that infernal Venus."

" You did not pull hard enough."

" Yes, indeed I did — But the Venus — she has bent her finger."

He stared at me wildly, and leaned against the window-sash to prevent himself from falling.

" What nonsense ! " I said. " You pushed the ring on too far. You can get it off to-morrow

with pincers.   But be careful not to damage
the statue."

" No, I tell you.   The Venus' finger is
crooked, bent under ; she clinches her hand,
do you hear me ? . . . She is my wife apparently, since I have given her my ring. . . . She
will not return it."

I shivered, and, for a moment, I was all
goose-flesh.   Then a great sigh from him
brought me a whiff of wine, and all my emotion
disappeared.

The wretch, I thought, is dead drunk.

" You are an antiquarian, sir," added the
bridegroom in a mournful tone ; " you understand those statues ; there is, perhaps, some
hidden spring, some deviltry which I do not
know about.   Will you go and see ? "

" Certainly," I replied.   " Come with me."

" No, I would prefer to have you go alone."

I left the drawing-room.

The weather had changed during supper,
and a heavy rain had begun to fall.   I was
about to ask for an umbrella, when a sudden
thought stopped me.   I should be a great fool,
I reflected, to go and verify what had been told
me by a drunken man !   Besides, he may have
wished to play some silly trick on me to give
cause for laughter to the honest country people ;
and the least that can happen to me from it is
to be drenched to the bone and catch a bad
cold.

From the door I cast a glance at the statue running with water, and I went up to my room without returning to the drawing-room. I went to bed ; but sleep was long in coming. All the scenes of the day passed through my mind. I thought of the young girl, so pure and love-ly, abandoned to a drunken brute. What an odious thing a marriage of convenience is ! A mayor dons a tri-colored scarf, a priest a stole, and then the most virtuous girl in the world is delivered over to the Minotaur! What can two people who do not love each other find to say at a moment, which two lovers would buy at the price of their lives ? Can a woman ever love a man whom she has once seen coarse ? First impressions are never effaced, and I am sure M. Alphonse will deserve to be hated.

During my monologue, which I abridge very much, I had heard a great deal of coming and going in the house. Doors opened and shut, and carriages drove away. Then I seemed to hear on the stairs the light steps of a number of women going towards the end of the hall opposite my room. It was probably the bride's train of attendants leading her to bed. After that they went down stairs again. Madame de Peyrehorade's door closed. How troubled and ill at ease that poor girl must be, I thought. I tossed about in my bed with bad temper. A bachelor plays a stupid part in a house where a marriage is accomplished.

Silence had reigned for some time when it was disturbed by a heavy tread mounting the stairs. The wooden steps creaked loudly.

"What a clown!" I cried to myself. "I wager that he will fall on the stairs." All was quiet again. I took up a book to change the current of my thoughts. It was the county statistics, supplemented with an address by M. de Peyrehorade on the Druidical remains of the district of Prades. I grew drowsy at the third page. I slept badly, and awoke repeatedly. It might have been five o'clock in the morning, and I had been awake more than twenty minutes, when the cock crew. Day was about to dawn. Then I heard distinctly the same heavy footsteps, the same creaking of the stairs which I had heard before I fell asleep. I thought it strange. Yawning, I tried to guess why M. Alphonse got up so early. I could imagine no likely reason. I was about to close my eyes again, when my attention was freshly excited by a singular trampling of feet, which was soon intermingled with the ringing of bells and the sound of doors opened noisily; then I distinguished confused cries.

"My drunkard has set something on fire," I thought, jumping out of bed. I dressed quickly and went into the hall. From the opposite end came cries and lamentations, and a heart-rending voice dominated all the others: "My son! my son!" It was evident that an accident had happened to M. Alphonse. I ran to the bridal apartment: it was full of people. The first sight which struck my gaze was the young man partly dressed and stretched across the bed, the wood-work of which was broken. He was livid and motionless. His mother sobbed and wept beside him. M. de Peyrehorade moved about frantically; he rubbed his son's temples with cologne water, or held salts to his nose. Alas! his son had long been dead. On a sofa at the other side of the room lay the bride, a prey to dreadful convulsions. She was making inarticulate cries, and two robust maid-servants had all the trouble in the world to hold her down. "Good heavens!" I exclaimed, "what has happened?"

I approached the bed and raised the body of the unfortunate young man: it was already stiff and cold. His clinched teeth and black face expressed the most fearful anguish. It was evident enough that his death had been violent and his agony terrible.

Nevertheless, no sign of blood was on his clothes. I opened his shirt, and on his chest I found a livid mark which extended around the ribs to the back. One would have said he had been squeezed in an iron ring. My foot touched something hard on the carpet; I stooped and saw it was the diamond ring. I dragged M. de Peyrehorade and his wife into their room, and had the bride carried there.

"You still have a daughter," I said to them. "You owe her your care." Then I left them alone.

To me it did not seem to admit of a doubt that M. Alphonse had been the victim of a murder whose authors had discovered a way to introduce themselves into the bride's room during the night. The bruises on the chest and their circular direction, however, perplexed me, for they could not have been made either by a club or an iron bar. Suddenly I remembered having heard that at Valencia *bravi* used long leather bags filled with sand to stun people whom they had been paid to kill. Immediately I thought of the Aragonese muleteer and his threat. Yet I hardly dared suppose he would have taken such a terrible revenge for a trifling jest.

I went through the house seeking everywhere for traces of house-breaking, but could find none. I descended to the garden to see if the assassins could have made their entrance from there; but there were no conclusive signs of it. In any case, the evening's rain had so softened the ground that it could not have retained any very clear impress. Nevertheless, I noticed some deeply marked footprints; they ran in two contrary directions, but on the same path. They started from the corner of the hedge next the racquet-court and ended at the door of the house. They might have been made by M. Alphonse when he went to get his ring from the finger of the statue. Then again, the hedge at this spot was narrower than elsewhere, and it must have been here that the murderers got over it. Passing and repassing before the statue, I stopped a moment to consider it. This time, I must confess, I could not contemplate its expression of vicious irony without fear; and, my mind being filled with the horrible scene I had just witnessed, I seemed to see in it a demoniacal goddess applauding the sorrow fallen on the house.

I returned to my room and stayed there till noon. Then I left it to ask news of my hosts. They were a little calmer. Mlle. de Puygarrig, or I should say the widow of M. Alphonse, had regained consciousness. She had even spoken to the *procureur du roi* from Perpignan, then in circuit at Ille, and this magistrate had received her deposition. He asked for mine. I told him what I knew, and did not hide from him my suspicions about the Aragonese muleteer. He ordered him to be arrested on the spot.

"Have you learned anything from Mme.

Alphonse ? " I asked the *procureur du roi* when my deposition was written and signed.

" That unfortunate young woman has gone crazy," he said, smiling sadly. " Crazy, quite crazy. This is what she says :

" She had been in bed for several minutes with the curtains drawn, when the door of her room opened and some one entered. Mme. Alphonse was on the inside of the bed with her face turned to the wall. Assured that it was her husband she did not move. Presently the bed creaked as if laden with a tremendous weight. She was terribly frightened, but dared not turn her head. Five minutes, or ten minutes perhaps — she has no idea of the time — passed in this way. Then she made an involuntary movement, or else it was the other person who made one, and she felt the contact of something as cold as ice, that is her expression. She buried herself against the wall trembling in all her limbs.

" Shortly afterwards, the door opened a second time, and some one came in who said, ' Good evening, my little wife.' Then the curtains were drawn back. She heard a stifled cry. The person who was in the bed beside her sat up apparently with extended arms. Then she turned her head and saw her husband, kneeling by the bed with his head on a level with the pillow, held close in the arms of a sort of

greenish-colored giant. She says, and she repeated it to me twenty times, poor woman ! —
she says that she recognized — do you guess
who? — the bronze Venus, M. de Peyrehorade's
statue. Since it has been here every one dreams
about it. But to continue the poor lunatic's
story. At this sight she lost consciousness,
and probably she had already lost her mind.
She cannot tell how long she remained in this
condition. Returned to her senses she saw the
phantom, or the statue as she insists on calling it, lying immovable, the legs and lower part
of the body on the bed, the bust and arms extended forward, and between the arms her hus-
· band, quite motionless. A cock crew. Then
the statue left the bed, let fall the body, and
went out. Mme. Alphonse rushed to the bell,
and you know the rest."

The Spaniard was brought in ; he was calm,
and defended himself with much coolness and
presence of mind. He did not deny the remark which I had overheard, but he explained
it, pretending that he did not mean anything
except that the next day, when rested, he
would beat his victor at a game of racquets.
I remember that he added :

" An Aragonese when insulted does not wait
till the next day to revenge himself. If I had
believed that M. Alphonse wished to insult me
I would have ripped him up with my knife on
the spot."

His shoes were compared with the footprints in the garden; the shoes were much the larger.

Finally, the innkeeper with whom the man lodged asserted that he had spent the entire night rubbing and dosing one of his mules which was sick. And, moreover, the Aragonese was a man of good reputation, well known in the neighborhood, where he came every year on business.

So he was released with many apologies.

I have forgotten to mention the statement of a servant who was the last person to see M. Alphonse alive. It was just as he was about to join his wife, and calling to this man he asked him in an anxious way if he knew where I was. The servant answered that he had not seen me. M. Alphonse sighed, and stood a minute without speaking, then he said : " Well! the devil must have carried him off also ! "

I asked the man if M. Alphonse had on his diamond ring. The servant hesitated; at last he said he thought not; but for that matter he had not noticed.

"If the ring had been on M. Alphonse's finger," he added, recovering himself, " I should probably have noticed it, for I thought he had given it to Mme. Alphonse."

When questioning the man I felt a little of the superstitious terror which Mme. Alphonse's statement had spread through the house. The *procureur du roi* smiled at me, and I was careful not to insist further.

A few hours after the funeral of M. Alphonse I prepared to leave Ille. M. de Peyrehorade's carriage was to take me to Perpignan. Notwithstanding his feeble condition, the poor old man wished to accompany me as far as the garden gate. We crossed the garden in silence, he creeping along supported by my arm. As we were about to part I threw a last glance at the Venus. I foresaw that my host, though he did not share the fear and hatred which it inspired in his family, would wish to rid himself of an object which must ceaselessly recall to him a dreadful misfortune. My intention was to induce him to place it in a museum. As I hesitated to open the subject, M. de Peyrehorade turned his head mechanically in the direction he saw I was looking so fixedly. He perceived the statue, and immediately melted into tears. I embraced him, and got into the carriage without daring to say a word.

Since my departure I have not learned that any new light has been thrown on this mysterious catastrophe.

M. de Peyrehorade died several months after his son. In his will he left me his manuscripts, which I may publish some day. I did not find among them the article relative to the inscriptions on the Venus.

P. S. — My friend M. de P. has just written to me from Perpignan that the statue no longer exists. After her husband's death Madame de Peyrehorade's first care was to have it cast into a bell, and in this new shape it does duty in the church at Ille. " But," adds M. de P., "it seems as if bad luck pursues those who own the bronze. Since the bell rings at Ille the vines have twice been frozen."

www.ingramcontent.com/pod-product-compliance
Lightning Source LLC
Chambersburg PA
CBHW030116030726
47498CB00007B/2416